Climax

by

Sexxa Kohl

Climax

by Sexxa Kohl

DISCLAIMER

This is a work of fiction. Names, characters, businesses, places, events and incidents are either the products of the author's imagination or used in a fictitious manner. Any resemblance to actual persons, living or dead, or actual events is purely coincidental.

ISBN-13: 978-1495947735
ISBN-10: 1495947734

Editor: Kathryn McNeill Crane, Indie Express LLC

Cover Rights © MGCover Design

Formatted by Lori Hall-Underwood

DEDICATION

To my sexy husband… My Master,

My body and soul are forever enslaved to you! I love you more than you will ever know. I look forward to many more years of being spanked by you.

-Sexxa

"Erotic passion lies enslaved within all of our souls. Never be afraid to unleash it!"

- Sexxa Kohl

*

"Sex is a part of nature. I go along with nature."

-Marilyn Monroe

*

"A dirty book is rarely dusty."

~Author Unknown

TABLE OF CONTENTS

MY SEXY ACKNOWLEDGEMENTS..i
PROLOGUE..v
CHAPTER ONE..1
CHAPTER TWO..7
CHAPTER THREE..15
CHAPTER FOUR..21
CHAPTER FIVE..31
CHAPTER SIX..41
CHAPTER SEVEN..43
CHAPTER EIGHT..51
CHAPTER NINE..67
CHAPTER TEN..75
CHAPTER ELEVEN..85
CHAPTER TWELVE..89
CHAPTER THIRTEEN..93
CHAPTER FOURTEEN..101
CHAPTER FIFTEEN..109
CHAPTER SIXTEEN..111
CHAPTER SEVENTEEN..113
CHAPTER EIGHTEEN..119
CHAPTER NINETEEN..123
CHAPTER TWENTY..129
CHAPTER TWENTY-ONE..133
CHAPTER TWENTY-TWO..141
CHAPTER TWENTY-THREE..147

CHAPTER TWENTY-FOUR 153
CHAPTER TWENTY-FIVE 159
CHAPTER TWENTY-SIX 165
CHAPTER TWENTY-SEVEN 171
CHAPTER TWENTY-EIGHT 175
CHAPTER TWENTY-NINE 179
CHAPTER THIRTY 187
CHAPTER THIRTY-ONE 199
EPILOGUE 203
NOTE FROM SEXXA 209
ABOUT SEXXA KOHL 211
CLIMAX PLAYLIST 213

MY SEXY ACKNOWLEDGEMENTS

Lots of research goes into writing any book. I wanted to be very thorough with Climax, so I spent LOTS of time tied up in bed with my delicious master. Through MANY hair pulling, teeth biting MULTIPLE orgasms, I rendered my research perfect and conclusive. And OH MY GOD the sex was just HOT! (Pronounced in my most heavy Southern accent: “HAWT”)

To My Master, I surrender to you. I’m enslaved to your body. You own me. Every single inch of my body begs for your command. Through the pain and madness, we find our love. I crave your touch as much as I do my next breath. You will forever be my lover, my best friend...my husband. You can tie me up and spank me anytime, baby. ANYTIME! (Now is great, as a matter of fact).

To my Fucking FABULOUS Hussy Betas and ARC Readers! What dirty little sluts you are!! I LOVE IT! I ADORE YOU ALL BEYOND WORDS! Work that pole honey!

Roll Call!

Bodacious Bex AKA Becky N.

Ginger Twist- AKA Amber V.

Kinki Kiki- AKA Kristina A.

Foxxy Love- AKA Cassandra K.

Tabby Staxx- AKA Tabitha W.

Lissa Lace-AKA Melissa G.

Melayna Ecstasy-AKA Joni P.

Juicy Jules-AKA Julie D.

Kami Sutra-AKA Michelle G.

Cherry Pop-AKA Jenna T.

Lola Sparkles-AKA Leanne M.

Fanny Noir-AKA Francesca C.

Moon Spitter-AKA Krystle L.

Midnight Angel-AKA Angela L.

Gigi j'adore-AKA Angela P.

Mistress Mystic-AKA Mia M.

Freekie Love-AKA Claudia J.

Sparkle Bitch-AKA April B.

My hookers, I can never begin to say thank you enough for taking the time to read my book. I hope it wet your panties and knickers ladies! I LOVE ALL OF YOU! Remember there is a stripper in all of us! Some of us more than others…AHEM*** "AIN'T NO SHAME…BABY DO YO THANG!"

My Dirty Little Whore Street Team, You ladies are the spice and driving force in helping me get Climax out there and in reader's hands! Thank you for taking the time and chance on me! Words can NEVER express my thanks for every single post, teaser, share, like, and message you send. I ADORE YOU ALL!!

MGBOOKCOVERS You fucking rock my world bitch! I told you HOT and you brought it! My cover is unbelievably sexy! I fucking love you Meli!!!!

FEISTY GIRLS BLOG: Joni, Meli & Mia, You girls are kick ass! You go out of your way to pimp me and there are NO WORDS to say "Thank You" for ALL your support!!!!! I MORE THAN FUCKING ADORE YOU!!! You are blessings in my life!

Katie Mac, My Bedazzled Sex Southern Goddess Editor AKA The Indie Express LLC, I can NEVER EVER say how MUCH I adore you! I worked hard to control my dot obsession this time, but sometimes Dotty comes out with a vengeance. You're like the most AWESOME Hussy I know and I treasure our friendship more than you will ever possibly know. Be on the lookout because I am totally thinking of writing unicorn porn now! Wine, chocolate, and orgasms are the three important ingredients in life baby!!!! Can't wait to kick it with you in Knoxville! I LOVE YOU!!

L.U. Ann (The Indie Express LLC) , my dirty little skank, OH HOW I LOVE YOU! You're emails kept my chin up and my side sore from laughing. When I told you what I imagined for graphics and formatting, you fucking nailed it! OMG!!!! You ROCK MY WORLD! You are my soul sister LULU!! MWAH!!!!

Harper Sloan Oh how I adore you babe! Thank you for taking the time to send me some INCREDIBLE pictures for Climax inspiration! Our hilarious conversations kept my side sore from laughing. I just love that dirty little mind of yours!! MWAH!

Nikki Sex & Kendall Grey, Thank you so much for your words of encouragement and the push to make the leap into the erotica world!! MWAH!

To my Facebook Felon, AKA Becky Carter Nichols You are my bitch! You're teasers for Climax are off the charts HOT! They were so HOT in fact, that you took one for the team and spent a little time in Facebook Jail for them!! When I needed inspiration, you filled me with jaw dropping pictures of delicious eye candy…and grandpa porn (****hurling****). Now know I must ALWAYS be cautious of my email picture attachments. YUCK! Did you like old Grandma there? DON'T MESS WITH THE QUEEN HUSSY! LOVE YA!!

PIMPSLAPPED Bex & Ambs there aren't enough words to tell you two how much I love you! Thank you for everything you have done for me! You both know how I like it so you can PIMPSLAP ME ANYTIME BABY!! Oh, and Ambs, I am still looking for those candy windows!

To Angela Page, My Eye Candy Pimp! What would I have ever done without my daily supply of deliciousness sent to my email? Thank you from the bottom of my heart for pushing me on the parts of Climax that needed more clarity. Through our mutual love of alcohol and handcuffs, our conversations have been quite enjoyable! Bowtie keeps me laughing! I swear he was a stripper in his past life!

Kristina Amit, My Dirty Little Angel Oh how you keep me smiling. I can never say just how much you mean to me! I love how you drunk text me baby!! You're such a sassy little minx! Remember, alcohol always makes EVERYTHING better! MWAH!

I love you!

Kaydee Mavericks, Riley Rhea, and Jenna Tyler, our late night chats keep me sane. Thank you for all the laughter and rude name calling. You girls are forever my skanks! MWAH!!!!

Krystle & Francesca, My Naughty Little Brits! You keep me smiling all the way across the globe. Since you apparently have no sun where you live, I hope you enjoy the moon! Be sure to keep your knickers out of a twist! LOVE YOU GUYS! “Cheerio there Lassies!“

To Jamie P. (AKA Moon Spitters baby daddy) Thank you for spitting on my girl’s back for her. That funny moment of your passion, inspired me to show you how it really can be done □. So drink lots of water, save up your spit, and be sure to try that scene out with Krystle! I think she MIGHT just enjoy the spitting better this time. Jamie, you might have just started a sexual revolution! LMAO!!

To the Prudes of the World… SEX IS GOOD! Get over yourself!

To My Readers, THANK YOU from the bottom of my slutty little heart for taking a chance on Climaxing with me! GO SPICE UP YOUR LIFE PEOPLE!! Be sure to be on the look out for Book 2 DOMINATE-Honey’s story!

PROLOGUE

If asked what I thought I would be doing at twenty-two, it certainly wouldn't be taking my clothes off for complete strangers. The world looks at me as both a whore and a worthless piece of trash, even though I only work here to pay for my mother's medical bills. No one would believe that I am still a virgin, waiting to find love. I can easily say that I don't think love is ever going to be finding me here at Club Climax.

As I stare out over the crowd, I give them what they want. For the next three and a half minutes of this song, I dance, undress, shake my ass, and slide up and down the metal pole in front of me. I control everything I do while I am up here on this stage. That is how it works at this place; I make the rules. That is, of course, except the room in the far back known as Ultimate Climax. All power is surrendered and lost there. I have promised myself that I will never go back there, no matter how desperate I get. The price is too high for me; I refuse to sell myself to the highest bidder. I cannot afford to lose the only thing I have left. My control.

There comes a time when we have to do the things that we said we would never do. For me, that day has finally arrived.

As I grab the handle of the door, I pause to take a deep breath. Once I walk through that door, my whole life will forever change. I will give up everything, and I pray that when I leave, I will have something left of myself.

Chapter One

Blaire

Rihanna's "Pour it Up" blares through the speakers of the room as I rock my body against the steel pole. The heavy bass pumps and blends with the loud catcalls and whistles of drunken men. I despise being here. Shutting my eyes, I close myself off to tune out their remarks. I have to. If I don't, I will end up running off this stage right now and hurling. After six months of doing this four times a week, a person should be used to it by now. But, I'm not. I will be damned if I ever let myself get used to this life.

As I said, you will find me here at least four nights a week. From eight o'clock at night until three o'clock in the morning, I'm known as Raven. Of course, Raven is just my stage name, but it fits me perfect when you consider my long, wavy ebony hair that I'd been blessed to inherit from my mom. No one here knows that my real name is Blaire Michaels, and I want to keep it that way. I've made nice with a couple of the girls that work here, but for the most part, I keep to myself. I deal with this shit a lot better that way.

At this place, friendships are virtually impossible, not to mention that it's too competitive. The girls here don't exactly like the fact that I am a crowd favorite. The only girl I really talk to is named Honey. As much as I want to know about the pain that I see in her eyes, I don't ask. She is the first one I met when I came to this club. She taught me the ropes and has never once acted as though I owe her anything. I wish we could be closer, but it's just not possible. Every little thing about working at Club Climax is based on half-truths and deceptive reality. I don't think anything good can actually come from that.

Once I walk out those back employee entrance doors, I switch back to Blaire Michaels, twenty-two-year old virgin, college drop out. Yes, I know what you are thinking. How can I be a virgin and a stripper? Well, believe it or not, I keep both my worlds private. It's a double-edged sword, really. Blaire and Raven both share pain either way they turn.

Don't judge me for what I do. My life might be easier to understand if I explain why I do this in the first place. My mom's mounting medical bills have forced me into this world.

Twelve years ago, she was diagnosed with mitral valve prolapse. Over the years, her condition has only worsened. A major episode with her heart last year forced her to stop working and stay at home.

Since the day my dad walked out on us when I was eight, it has been just her and me against the world. With no one else to care for her, I chose to drop out of college in the middle of my senior year to come help. Despite her pleas for me to finish school, I could never go back when she so desperately needed me here.

When I got home, how badly things had gotten out of hand for her both financially and physically surprised me. Bills were mounting up, and I found out that she had chosen to pay things like the light bill instead of buying her heart medications. Her little disability check received each month barely covered basic expenses, let alone medicines and food. She simply could not do this on her own.

No matter how many jobs I took, or how many hours I spent working, I never seemed to get us caught up. Last spring, the bank foreclosed on the only home I had ever known. When I looked around here for places to rent, I quickly found there were no decent places that I could afford. I needed to find a way to make some money fast because my bartending & waitressing jobs were not going to cut it. A flyer posted on our board at the bar where I worked led me here to Club Climax.

I will never forget the first time I walked into Club Climax. Immediately upon entering, it both thrilled and disgusted me. Seeing the way the girl moved on stage was erotic, but watching the way the men behaved when she glided up and down that pole in front of them disgusted me. When her performance was over, and I saw how much money she scooped up off the floor, I realized I had to bury my fears and do this. I had no other choice.

Who would have known on the day I started doing this that I'd be such a natural at it? Standing at five feet ten, I have all the voluptuous curves in just the right places. Add in my long, tone legs, and a very busty top and I more than pass the criteria for getting a job at this kind of place. Here at the club, I flaunt my beauty and assets, but when I walk out that door and back into Blaire's world, I'm as shy, self-conscious, and quiet as it comes. No one would ever know how hard this is for me to pretend to be something that I am not. It seems I have an on and off switch that I can flip in order to change whom I need to be for my basic survival.

I know exactly what men want when I am performing, and nothing will stop me from giving it to them. I work the stage, tempting them as I slowly strip and grind my body against the steel pole. They beg to see my ass, so I turn around and bend over, giving them a clear view of my black thong as I continue removing the tight shorts from my body. Whistles increase in volume and dollar bills fly up on stage. Scanning the floor, I quickly assess how much is there before I give them any more.

Shit! Only about fifty bucks.

Needing to kick it up a notch, I turn around, lean back against the pole, and shimmy down to the floor. Once I am on my knees, I crawl down the center of the stage where no one can reach or touch me. With each slow movement, my tits bounce up and down but remain tightly shoved and restrained in my corset. Near the edge of the stage, I shake my ass and my chest before sitting upright and lifting my long hair up above my head. Green bills fly around me as I spread my legs open and lean back onto the cold floor.

I fucking swear that if I hear, "Yeah, Baby," one more time, I am going to kill someone!

I stand and strut over to the pole. This part is what I hate and dread the most, the part where I give them everything I have. With my back to the crowd, I turn and arch my back against the pole while I unfasten the clasp in the front. With one forceful tug, I am free and thoroughly exposed. I drop the black corset on the floor and cover my breasts with my arm. The crowd goes wild as I prepare for my finale. Bass pumps in the speakers as loudly as my heart does in my chest.

You can do this, Blaire. You have to.

I wait for the perfect moment in the song, and then I spin around and drop my hand, baring everything to them. Green bills fly everywhere when I jump up to grab hold of the pole. I grind my crotch against the metal seductively as I climb high above the audience. I hold on tightly while I extend my legs out in a spread eagle position. Dirty, raunchy comments reach my ears even from all the way up here. Leaning backwards, I maneuver myself upside down and perform the crowd's favorite death drop. Every time I do this, it scares the shit out of me. I have learned the move by watching a lot of videos on pole dancing and visiting other clubs in my spare time. No one else here at Club Climax does it.

I flip my body over and touch my heels to the stage to stand. With perfect timing, the music ends just as I place my hands on my hips. The crowd is standing and continues to throw money at me while the announcer's voice echoes throughout the club's PA system.

"LET'S HEAR IT FOR OUR BABY GIRL … R-A-V-E-N!"

I reach down and scoop up my money while the bouncers guard the stage around me. Normally, I would never dare a glimpse out at anyone in the room, but tonight, for some unknown reason, I am drawn to do so.

I can't explain it. It is a feeling of need and desire mixed with an electrical wave of energy. Like a magnet, his glare immediately pulls me to him. I hold the money against my chest and can't move. My chest hurts as if the breath has just been sucked out of me. Honey is grinding her ass into his lap while he tightly grips her hips, but his eyes are firmly glued to mine. Regardless of his devastatingly handsome face, the fact he is here in this club tells me everything I need to know. Men like him are nothing but trouble; they use girls like Honey and me as if we are disposable garbage.

His heated eyes seductively travel down my body to my legs and then back up to my eyes. Fucking hell, how does he do that to me with just those dark eyes? Feeling the heat rise to my face, I break our intense stare and look down at the steps to exit the stage. Daring one last look into his dark blazing eyes, I discover something I don't want to know about myself. I like the lustful way he looks at me. That's too dangerous; it can bring nothing but more trouble and heartbreak into my already troubled and broken life.

Chapter Two

Jaxxon

I don't normally come into places like this, but for some reason, I am drawn here tonight. Finding a woman is never hard for a guy like me. I'm extremely good looking, in great shape, and more than blessed in size if you know what I mean. I've fucked more women than most guys could ever dream about. Of course, it doesn't hurt matters that I have more money than I could spend in ten lifetimes, family money earned by my Grandfather who designed and engineered one of the first artificial hearts. Ryder Technology is well known across the world for providing some of the most highly advanced products in the health care world today. It is a billion dollar industry, and our family has done quite well in conquering it over the years. I have grown up in luxury you wouldn't believe.

Women are like vultures when they smell that you have money. They like the shopping sprees, luxurious vacations, fancy cars, and jewelry. It's become an acquired taste to my lifestyle, and I hate when woman become possessive of me. When I am done, I am done. I'm not into loving relationships, and I'm sure as fuck not ever marrying anyone. The entire concept of marriage is a joke. The idea of having just one pussy for the rest of my life makes me laugh. My own parents have been married for twenty-seven years, and both have fucked around since the day they said, "I do"! I admire loyalty and commitment, but I like to decide when that begins and ends. That is why I prefer Dominant/submissive relationships over random fucking, but when the need hits, I will choose a quick, meaningless fuck any day to temporarily feed my desire.

That's part of the reason I am here. Club Climax offers me the ability to mix both BDSM and random fucking. Tonight I need both of those things.

The term making love always makes me laugh. There is no need to involve romance in sex. Sex. Fucking. They are both the same. Sex is supposed to be hard, fast, and raw. Why would anyone want to take his time and be slow and sweet? There is no reason to consider the other person's feelings. I admit it. I am a selfish creature. I only care about my own pleasure, my own gain.

I take what I want.

I take what I need.

Control.

I need this way of life. To me, it's as vital as breathing. Something about the way a woman totally yields her power drives me absolutely insane with a ruthless hunger that desperately needs to be fed. It's insatiable. I demand everything from them; they will get nothing from me in return. Even their pleasure is mine to decide. The fate is held in my hands.

Darkness fills my soul. I am cold, callous, and evil.

I don't love.

I don't care.

It's the man I am. It's whom I have been made to become. I decide whom I bring into my life; I decide how long they stay there.

Growing up, I never had control, and I certainly never had a voice in anything. I saw how my father treated people around him. I wanted people to look at me the way he demanded them to look at him. Maybe then, he'd see the imaginary boy who begged his whole life to be seen.

Even at an early age, our maids and assistants frequented my bedroom. I treated them with just as much disrespect as my father showed me. It only made me ravenous for more. An early taste of BDSM opened my eyes to a world where only I rule.

There is no room in my world for anyone.

I don't need anyone to care for me.

The Ultimate Climax room is legendary around here. It comes at a hefty price, but money is not an issue with me. Places like this allow me to get my fix without worries of attachment. These women aren't clingy; they can't be. It's business for them, pure and simple. You give them the money, and they give you their time. I both like and respect them for it, regardless of the fact that most of these women have fucked half the town.

I walk inside and see the sly smiles of the girls as they turn to face my way. I will say that most of the girls here are pretty fucking hot. Whistles and screams fill the room, along with loud music that blares around me. Spotting an open table up ahead, I glimpse the seductive movement of a girl in the background. I don't even look at her at first because I am too busy looking for my hookup for the night. I spot a hot brunette eyeing me as she pulls on a sucker in her mouth. She makes her way over and stands in front of me, fully blocking my view of the stage. I don't honestly care. If you've seen one pole dance, you've seen them all, right?

"Welcome to Club Climax, I'm Honey. Can I get you a drink, or perhaps you'd like a dance?" she says in a sexy southern accent. She returns the sucker in her mouth and rolls it around, tightly sucking in her cheeks.

Fuck, she is hot!

"I'll have both. Whiskey's fine." I throw a fifty at her.

She picks up the money, leaves to get my drink, and twisting her sumptuous ass to the bar, leans in to give the bartender my order. My cock pushes hard against my zipper, so I move to adjust my pants.

Yeah, she might be just what I need tonight.

Suddenly, the crowd goes crazy, and my attention leaves Honey as I turn to look at the stage.

Holy fucking hell!

A goddess is now standing before me. Her long, black waves

cascade down her shoulders and frame her beautiful face. Her huge tits bounce free from her hold when she drops her hands and shows the crowd. Her hourglass figure sports a perfectly flat, toned tummy and slim waist. Black stilettos only make her long luscious legs look even longer, leading up to her perfectly sinful, round ass.

Sweet Jesus!

My cock throbs in my pants when she pushes her ass into the steel pole. It's as if I can already feel her hot pussy folds sliding up and down on my shaft. Mesmerized, I watch her climb the metal pole up high into the air. Her strong arms hold her in place while she opens her legs wide into the splits, giving the crowd a glimpse of the tiny fabric covering her opening.

Images of her bound to my bed make me smile. I want my mouth right there between her thighs. I want to be drenched in her sweet pussy juices while I torture her with pleasure. I can see her attached to my St. Andrew's cross, panting with need and desire, begging me to let her come. My dick stretches against the denim of my jeans even more when I imagine the skin on that delectable ass of hers glowing blood red from the spanking of my crop.

I need her.

I want her.

I will have her.

The men gasp and cheer when she drops upside down on the pole. I pay close attention to the way she squeezes her firm thighs to the steel in order to catch herself before she reaches the floor. Honey returns with my drink, and picks the perfect time to sit down on my lap and grind her ass against me.

"Already ready for me, huh." She leans back into me, rocking her hips back and forth.

My eyes never leave the beauty on the stage. I grip Honey's hips and press my hardness up against her crotch. She moans loudly before leaning back against me and increasing her thrusts. She thinks she is getting me off, but in reality, I'm only using her body while I visualize the temptress on the stage. She is whom I want, not Honey.

"LET'S HEAR IT FOR OUR BABY GIRL … R-A-V-E-N!" The announcer screams into the microphone.

Raven.

The name fits her perfectly. She senses someone staring at her. Confused, she looks up and glances across the room. Her eyes lock onto mine, and the breath leaves my chest. My eyes roam her body and take in every detail, scanning for anything that I might have missed before. She holds the money tightly against her, almost as if she is embarrassed.

Why is she doing that?

Most strippers aren't modest, so this is mind-blowing to me. She breaks our stare and moves to step off the platform. I know she saw Honey grinding on me, but to be honest, I don't think about that right now. I want her to look at me again. As if I have willed her to my command, she turns and shoots me another glance. This time I see hurt in her eyes. She blinks and turns to walk backstage.

Normally, hurt is the last fucking thing I care about. I've sent many girls out the door the minute I see tears. Girly emotions are not my thing. I've been taught to respect people, but I've also never been allowed to feel anything. I've been loved, but I've never been in love. It's who I am and who I will always be. For some reason, with this girl, it's different. I don't want to see the hurt in her eyes. The pain I wish to give her is pleasuring, not like this. I can't understand why the hell I even care, but I do.

I shove Honey off my lap and stand to go after Raven. Honey pulls at my arm and leans in to whisper into my ear.

"Take me to Ultimate Climax and we can have some fun."

The only person I'm taking into that room is Raven, and I'm headed to get her right now.

"No, thanks." I throw her another fifty. She nods and smiles at me, but I just grab my coat and head to the door that leads backstage.

A dickhead bouncer stops me at the door.

"Sorry, no one is allowed backstage."

"I would like to request the girl that just left the stage. I believe her name is Raven." I shove a bill in his hand in hopes of convincing him to be helpful.

"Raven, huh?" His face breaks out into a wide, wicked smile. Something about the look in his eyes makes me instantly want to punch him in the face.

What the fuck is going on with me? She is just a fucking stripper.

"Yeah, well, our girl Raven is a tough one. She doesn't do the floor or the room. She just dances twice a night, and that's it. You just caught her first performance. She'll be up in another hour or so. I'm sure some other girl will be happy to keep you occupied until then."

"I'm sure they can, but I would like to speak to her," I demand through gritted teeth. This motherfucker is pissing me off. He doesn't know what he is up against.

"Look dude, you'll have to wait like the rest of them in here do and try talking to her then. Our Raven draws big crowds in on the nights she works. She's the only one of the girls here that performs twice in the same night, but if you're thinking you're going to get some, she don't put out. I know I've tried." He snickers and I smell the stench of his breath.

I don't give him the satisfaction of a response. If I do, he will be on the floor.

I growl under my breath. I am not used to being told no or not getting my way when I want something. Walking back over to my table, I grab up my untouched whiskey. Throwing it back, I embrace the burn as it makes its way down my throat. The bouncer still has me seething with anger, so I move towards the bar and motion for another round.

Suddenly, the bartender yells a girl's name, bringing me out of my daze.

"Lacey! Boss said he wants Raven up before you tonight. Go tell her for me."

The girl nods her head and turns to leave.

I reach out and grab her by the arm before she can move any farther.

“I need you to give Raven something when you go back there, please,” I say while taking a pen off the bar and writing on the back of one the club’s business cards. Jotting down a ridiculous number, I hand it to the girl and prepare to finally get my way in that back room with Raven tonight.

I sit back, turn up the rest of my drink, and smile. She would be a fool to turn down that amount of money. No one turns down Jaxxon Ryder.

Chapter Three

Blaire

I can't explain the raging jealousy that I'm feeling right now. Honey is my friend, yet all I can think about is how she had been grinding herself against the beautiful man. The same beautiful man that I want. Guys like him come in here all the time, so why is he affecting me this way? It is obvious that he is here for one thing only, and he has found it in Honey's crotch.

Not wanting to face her when she comes backstage, I decide to get ready early for my next set. To get through tonight, I just need to avoid her. I am sure that I'll get over it soon enough.

This must just be an off night for me.

My shiny white and silver corset laces tightly in the back shoving my tits up so high in the front that I swear they are going to pop out and smack me in the face. After securing the last fastener in the front, I change into the matching white lace thong with garter belt and white hose. Once I am done, I step into my silver stilettos and check my appearance in the long mirror on the wall. The old mirror has a huge crack down the middle from where a bouncer angrily punched it last month. The split in the glass distorts my image, and ironically, I can relate to what it represents. I am staring at two different people, Raven and Blaire. What a divided, broken life we both share.

This angel costume is not only my pick, but also a favorite of the crowd's, too. I need big tips tonight, so I'm pulling all stops with this one. I have a while to wait, so I decide to hold off attaching my wings until I go out on stage.

Honey is performing, so I make my way over to my section of the long dressing room table and sit. I style my hair in a sexy upsweep and secure my long, dark locks with a silver hairpin. The guys love it when I remove the pin and shake my loose, long curls down my back. It is a guaranteed moneymaker.

I'm freshening up my makeup when Lacey yells my name from across the room.

"Raven! Mike says you're dancing before me tonight!" she informs me before turning to talk to another girl coming into the room. Great! I am not ready to go back out there just yet. I close my eyes and try to calm my nerves, but then Lacey's voice startles me.

"Hey, I almost forgot. This guy asked me to give you this." She hands me what looks to be one of Club Climax's business cards. I flip it over and read what is written on the back.

Ultimate Climax

$5000

Mr. R

What the hell? This guy is seriously offering five grand just for one night with me? Is this guy crazy?

As I toss the card back on the counter in front of me, Lacey searches my face in the mirror for a reaction.

"Are you seriously going to say no to that? No girl here has even gotten an offer for half that amount. Mike sure wastes a lot of time on your ass by keeping you here. You are nothing but a cock tease!" Lacey bitterly spits out at me.

"Here, you want it so much then you take it. I'm not interested, so go for it!" I offer the card to her and stand to get ready for my set.

“Are you serious?” she asks me, wide eyed in shock.

“Yep. Go for it.”

She jerks the card out of my hand and squeals in delight, before turning back around to face me.

“Can you tell Mike that I won’t be going on after you? Be sure to tell him that I am taking the room offer instead.”

I nod my head and roll my eyes as she runs out the door.

“Ten minutes, Raven, and you’re up,” the bouncer yells to me from the doorway.

Hurriedly, I stand to go put on my wings, but they are not hanging in my wardrobe section.

Damn it!

I remember that I let Honey borrow my wings for one of her sets last week. She never returns anything she borrows. I hurry to her section of clothes, but the wings are not there.

Looking up at the clock, I know I only have a few minutes before I have to take the stage. I dig in the pile of clothes that she has shoved in the back. *SHIT!* Honey is one of the messiest girls back here, and I should have known better than to lend her the wings in the first place. I spot the white, furry fabric of a wing and snatch it up, silently praying that the other wing isn’t broken. Thankfully, it is only a little scuffed, so I hurry and slide my arms through the laces. Running down the hall, I barely make it to the platform in time for my introduction.

“And here is our beautiful angel who is here to save us all. Let’s give up for R-A-V-E-N!”

The lights drop and I take my place on stage in complete darkness as Massive Attack’s “Angel” begins hauntingly playing in the room. Slowly, a soft light illuminates around me as I slide my back down the pole. Swaying my hips back and forth, I face away from the crowd and slowly bend forward to expose my ass to them. Turning, I walk to the center of the stage like I usually do for my angel performance. This time, I am drawn to the table where Beautiful Man sat earlier tonight. It’s so dark that I can’t make out if he is sitting there or if it is someone else. Either way, my eyes are locked in that direction.

The slow music builds, but instead of performing the rest of this number on the pole, I find myself slowly and seductively stripping for the table in front of me. Normally, I am working the stage and giving the men my attention, but for some reason tonight, I dance only for him, Beautiful Man, and hope he is still watching me.

Unclasping my corset, I drop it to the ground and sink to my knees. The music pumps the bass again as I reach and unclasp my hairpin, allowing my long, black waves to spill down my back. Spreading my legs for him, I do the unthinkable. I run my hand down into my panties and then arch my back to the pleasure it suddenly brings me. Green bills fly in the air around me, but I only think about the one man I want to see this. Bringing my wet fingers to my mouth, I suck on them and hear the crowd scream in delight. When the music finishes and the lights fade to dark, I sit there, shocked at what I've just done.

What the fuck is wrong with me? Am I totally losing it?

Grabbing the money and shoving it in my bag, I step off stage and slip into the silk robe that is waiting for me. Behind me, I hear the guys still whistling. I hurriedly make my way backstage where I am met by an extremely angry Lacey.

She pushes past me and nearly knocks me on my ass.

"Get out of my way!" She screams at the other girls in the room while she makes her way to her dressing closet.

She storms back over to where I am and throws the card in my face.

"He told me he wasn't interested in me. Can you believe that shit? It seems he only wants you in that room. What a fucking waste you are to this place! How can you be okay with taking your clothes off, but not all right with working the floor like we do? Do you think that makes you any better than the any of us? I got news for you, bitch. You are just as dirty and slutty as we are."

Her words sting, but they are half-true. I am dirty, but I'm not a bitch. We all have our reasons for being here. Drug addiction, sexual pleasure, supporting a kid, and saving for my mom's surgery. Whatever reason, we are all here doing this to make a dollar. It isn't about what we do to make the dollar, but how we choose to spend that dollar that makes us different.

Shoving my bag full of my stuff, I quickly throw on a hoodie and a pair of sweat pants. Funny, I had been almost entirely naked a few moments ago, and now, virtually every inch of skin is covered. I grab my keys and head out of the back hallway. I need to tell Mike that I'm leaving early, so I knock on his door and hear a muffled moan.

Great! I guess he's in there banging another chick.

Refusing to let it get to me, I shove the door open as I speak, "Mike, I'm leav–," but my mouth drops at the sight in front of me. Honey is on her knees with her lips locked tightly around Beautiful Man's cock as he fists her hair in his hands. Leaning back against Mike's desk, his head is thrown back with his eyes closed. The pleasure on his face is undeniable. Suddenly, his dark eyes open and lock onto mine. Immediately, his face drops.

I stumble back against the wall, catching myself before I fall on my face. Bolting out of the room, I run down the hall and make my way out of the back exit door. As I make a mad dash for my car, tears sting my eyes. Fumbling my keys, I somehow manage to unlock the door and toss my bag in the back. Angrily, I hit the steering wheel of my old, blue Camry before collapsing my head onto my arms and crying.

I feel myself being drawn to look up, and when I raise my head, he is standing there in the parking lot staring back at me. I start my car and barrel out of the space, screeching my tires as I speed onto the highway. I don't know what the hell is going on with me tonight, but I have to get out of here and fast. I'm just relieved I don't have to be back at the club until next week. Right now, I just need to go home, check on my momma, and crawl into bed. But more than anything, I just need to be Blaire.

Jaxxon

I sit over at the bar and turn up my fourth drink while closely watching the backstage door for Raven to emerge. When the door finally opens, I spot Lacey, the girl I'd sent in earlier, coming my way with the card in her hand and a huge smile on her face.

"Hey there, so um … Raven says that she is not feeling up to this tonight." She hands me back the card. None of what she is saying makes any sense at all. I mean, how can any stripper not be interested in that kind of money? I know for a fact that my offer is at least ten times what anyone else pays for using that room.

"If you are looking for a wild time in Ultimate Climax, I assure you that I am the girl to choose," she purrs seductively while tracing her fingers down my arm.

Pulling my arm back, I give her a forced grin before answering.

"I am only interested in Raven."

Her face fills with anger, and she narrows her eyebrows at me.

"Just so you know, Raven never goes into that room with anyone. So you'll be beating a dead horse if it's her that you want," she snarls before storming off.

Wow, what a bitch!

Suddenly, the announcer begins to introduce the next act. When I hear her name, my heart begins racing and my dick begins throbbing. Looking around the room, I notice how packed the place has gotten in the last hour. I glance over at the table that I sat at earlier and notice that it is now occupied. I opt to move to the far back of the room to watch her perform.

Seductive music begins playing, and even though the stage remains pitch dark, I can make out her silhouette as she moves closer to the pole. Suddenly, a bright spotlight glows on the angelic creature on stage, knocking the mere breath from my chest.

She's so unbelievably gorgeous!

Whistles and vulgar comments fill the air as she slides her back down the metal pole before bending over to display her ass. Slowly, she turns and moves to the center of the stage, swaying her delicious hips as she moves.

Fuck me! That outfit is killing me.

Her eyes become fixated on the place where I had been sitting earlier tonight. Immediately, I begin hoping that she is looking for me. I know she can't see anyone out here in the crowd because the lights on stage are much too bright.

With one hand, she pulls on the front of her corset, freeing her heavy, full breasts. Scanning her gorgeous body, I drink every part of her sinful perfection in with my eyes. Suddenly, she drops to her knees and rocks her hips to the music, grinding down harder on the surface of the floor. Sitting back up, she raises her hand to her hair and releases a clasp of some sort, allowing her shiny long black waves to cascade down her back. As she arches her back again, her hands slide down in between her legs, making my cock press even harder against my zipper.

Holding my breath, I watch her hand as it slowly disappears into the front of her panties. With her legs spread wider for the crowd, she presses upwards on her hips to roll them to the beat of the music. Raven then raises her head to look again at the table in front of her. Inching her hand out, she eases her fingers up to her mouth. Mesmerized, I watch as her red lips seal around them and her jaw muscles draw in to suck. Instantly, I feel as if I am about to blow a load in my jeans.

The men go nuts at her antics and move toward the platform. This causes a frenzy amongst the bouncers, who push them away from the stage. Money flies from every direction around her. All I want to do is charge the stage and take her right there. I don't give a flying fuck who watches, I just want her. The desire, the need to have her is almost unbearable.

Finally, the song ends and the lights dim again. When she leaves the stage, I find myself angry and horny as fuck.

Who does she think she is turning me down? Better yet, how dare she tease me with that dance!

Closing my eyes, all I can think about is Raven pleasuring herself in front of me.

Fuck her! No woman is worth this!

I open my eyes and spot Honey in the corner. Pushing people aside, I make my way over and slam my lips to hers, taking her by surprise. I shove her against the wall and grab her ass, pulling her into my hardness. Looking into my eyes, she knows exactly what I want. She begins working feverishly to unbuckle my belt and looks over her shoulder at the hallway next to us.

"Come with me," she whispers into my ear.

Taking my hand, she pulls me back into the hallway and then shoves me into a room. When I look around, I notice we are in some sort of office, but I don't give a fuck. Right now, I need my cock sucked, and I don't give a damn whose room this is. Honey licks her lips and drops to her knees, pulling my jeans and boxer briefs down with her. Her hand firmly wraps around my long shaft, and I watch as she slyly grins back up at me. It is more than obvious that she likes what she sees.

Frantically, she begins pumping my hardness in her hands. I lean back and brace myself against the desk behind me as she leans in to take me into her mouth. Right now, the desperation is so intense that I need it hard and quick. Grabbing a fist full of her hair, I shove her head down harder onto my cock, urging her to take the full length in her mouth.

She may as well know now that there will be nothing gentle

about this tonight.

Raven floods my mind and I grow harder than before. I close my eyes to enjoy the warm tight vacuum on my cock. Even as her mouth sucks me off, I envision another. Raven. Just like earlier, Honey is only a means to fulfill a raging desire.

Out of nowhere, the door flies open, and I hear a girl let out a gasp. Lifting my head, I meet Raven's dark eyes. Honey never stops working my cock, and I'm too shocked right now to move or push her away. Raven covers her mouth with her hand and stumbles backwards into the wall behind her before running from the room.

"Get the fuck off me!" I push Honey, sending her on her ass. She wipes her mouth with the back of her hand and cusses me while I pull up my jeans. Throwing a wad of money at her, I rush out of the room.

I have to find her.

I catch a glimpse of her dark hair flowing as she runs out the front door of the club. When I finally get out onto the parking lot, I see her in her car with her head down on the steering wheel. Her shoulders shake, and I can tell that she is crying, all because of me. Normally, I would never give a fuck if a girl walked in on me while I was with someone else, but she is different. Thing is, what makes her different? For some reason, we are drawn to one another. This means far more than either of us could ever comprehend. Honestly, it leaves me scared shitless.

Sensing someone is watching, she lifts her head and locks onto my intense stare down. I stand there silently pleading with her, but then she slams on the gas and flies past me out of the parking lot. As I watch her taillights fade in the distance, I know that my life has just changed in a way I never thought possible.

She can fight it all she wants, but Raven will be mine.

Blaire

I wake up panting from yet another dream about the man at the club. My skin glistens with sweat, and my hand is still firmly tucked inside my panties, soaked with my pleasure. Just thinking again about the erotic dream I just woke from has me instantly blushing. I don't know what has come over me lately; it's as if I am not even myself anymore.

Four days have passed since that night, and I still can't get him out of my mind. I thought that if I focused on caring for my mom, the past few days would have been enough to keep my mind busy. But instead, he invades every possible thought and dream that I have. In the business I'm in, I can't afford for feelings like these to get in the way. He is just like any other guy that comes into that place. He's there to get his fix any way he can. Honey just happened to be the fix that he wanted and got that night.

Speaking of which, I have no clue how I am going to face Honey at work tonight. Unfortunately, calling off isn't an option that I have. I desperately need the money, so I don't have a choice. Besides, it isn't as if she even did anything wrong in the first place. This is all about my stupid, unwarranted jealousy. It sounds silly to admit, but in my mind, it's as if he has cheated on me with her. He is a stranger, for crying out loud. How fucked up in the head does that make me?

Since my mind is racing with thoughts of him, I know there isn't any way that I'm going to be able to go back to sleep. Throwing the thick comforter back, I decide to go ahead and get up to check on my mom.

Yesterday, her color bothered me so much that I ended up calling her doctor. Dr. Landers assured me that it was a normal part of her heart condition and told me to watch her closely, but not to worry.

Not worry? Is he freaking serious?

Worrying is all I ever do when it comes to my mom and my life. I'd love to be reminded of what it feels like to be laid back and carefree, even for just a day. Somehow, I don't think The Fairy Godmother or Prince Charming is coming to rescue this fair maiden.

Happily ever after's are fairy tales all in themselves; they are never meant for someone like me.

The sun is barely peeking through the blinds when I pad my way through the living room, over to where her hospital bed is located. The doctor had ordered her a special bed late last year to elevate her enough to help with her breathing. She hates not being able to sleep in her own soft bed, but she and I both know there isn't a choice in the matter.

Her labored breathing can be heard from across the room and immediately sends fear through my body. Every day, I watch her health decline more and more to the point where surgery is now her only option. A very complex surgery that we don't have enough money for. Without a huge percentage of the fee down, the heart specialists won't even consider her. Even though I have managed to save a couple thousand dollars, it won't even touch the amount requited to put her on their waiting list.

Lovingly, I brush back her hair and watch her sleep. This woman has done so much for me over the years. Since my dad ran out on us, she's managed to do it all on her own. The thought of losing her is just too much for me, and I fight against the tears that burn my eyes. She is all I have in this world; I will do anything I have to do in order to keep her here with me. If that means stripping in front of a bunch of strange men, then that will just be what it means.

Honestly, I feel horrible when I lie to my mother about what I do for a living. She thinks I work nights for a doctor's office filing records and doing bookkeeping. If you count the naughty nurse outfit at the club, I guess that could be considered something in the medical field. She will be devastated if she ever discovers that I take my clothes off for money. I can't risk her ever finding out because her heart is simply too weak to be able to handle the news.

As quietly as possible, I make my way into the adjoining kitchen to fix us both some breakfast. Glancing in the refrigerator and cabinets, I notice how low we have gotten on groceries. I've been so worried to leave her these past few days that I've not gone shopping. Looking up at the clock, I realize that her home health nurse, Elizabeth, will be here in a few hours. She only comes in twice a week for an hour, but it helps me out when our neighbor can't sit with her. I will have to take advantage of the hour she is here and run to the store. Our kind, elderly neighbor watches her for me while I am at work, and I buy her groceries in exchange for her kindness. It helps both of us since I know she is on a fixed income.

I scramble some eggs and toast before pouring us some juice. My mom loves raspberry jam, so I always make sure to spread on a lot when I make her breakfast. She is still sleeping soundly when I walk over and set her food down before sitting on the edge of her bed. I gently nudge her arm, but she's very hesitant to open her eyes. I reposition the oxygen tube back underneath her nose and force a smile when she finally opens her eyes. It breaks my heart to see such a wonderful woman struggle this way. I just want my mom back and healthy again.

"Hey, sweetie," she rasps in a weak, scratchy voice before rewarding me with a smile.

"Morning, Mom. How are you feeling?" I ask even though I know she isn't going to tell me the truth.

"I'm fine, Baby. Just a little tired, that's all," she replies weakly.

Turning away, I reach over to get her breakfast so that she won't see the tears that threaten to fall from my face. She grabs my fingers and stops me. I am surprised by her strength when she squeezes my hand. Swallowing the lump in my throat, I dare a look back into her beautiful green eyes.

Oh how I wish I had inherited the color of her eyes instead of my deadbeat father's.

"Blaire, Baby, don't worry about me. I'm gonna be all right. These doctors don't always know everything, you know."

Her words rip through me. I should be the one comforting her, not the other way around.

"You look so tired, Blaire. Why don't you go lie back down and rest? You have to work tonight, don't you?" She barely gets the words out before breaking into a terrible coughing spell.

Watching her as she tries to catch her breath makes me cringe. Even the slightest coughing fit can weaken her heart that much more. When it finally passes, I give her a sip of juice and hand her the plate of food before answering her.

"I'm fine, Mom. I just didn't sleep very well last night. Don't worry about me."

"Young lady, I'll be worrying about you until the day I die."

And there it is again. The thought of her not being here anymore. I can't hold it in this time. I have to get out of here. I quickly walk towards the bathroom.

"I'm going to get a shower before Elizabeth gets here." I walk into the small room, shutting the door behind me and turn on the water to drown out my crying. As I sit on the edge of the bathtub to let it all out, I realize that I can't pretend to be strong for much longer. I am barely holding on as it is.

By the time I shower and dress, I have managed to compose myself enough to face my mom again. Elizabeth meets me in the kitchen with a concerned look on her face.

"Blaire, your mom's oxygen level is extremely low this morning. I bumped up her intake on the machine, but that rattle in her chest has me terribly concerned. I put a call into Dr. Landers to discuss it with him. I should hear back within the hour of what he wants to do."

Nodding at her, I reply, "I know. I've stayed here with her these past few days because I've been afraid to leave her alone. I need to run to the store to pick up a few things. I should be back in about thirty minutes. Will you be alright until I get back?"

"Sure, sweetie, I'll watch her closely."

I thank her and turn to grab my jacket.

"Please call me if the doctor calls you before I get back." I say grabbing my keys.

"I will," she replies.

I go back into the living room to tell my mom goodbye, but she has already fallen back asleep. Tenderly, I kiss her on the forehead and try not to start crying when I feel how cold her skin is against my lips.

Please Mom, keep holding on!

I've been standing in this long checkout line for over fifteen minutes, and it hasn't moved an inch. Looking around the other shoppers, I notice the owner's son trying to fix the register. I spot the vintage clock on the wall and realize the time. Shit! I only have ten minutes, and there is no way I can get through this line in time.

Finally, the line begins moving, and I breathe a sigh of relief. I'm still going to be late, but hopefully I can make it back before Elizabeth has to leave. Just as I reach the counter, my phone rings, and I see that it is the nurse. She must be calling with news from the doctor.

Swiping the screen, I answer while I unload my groceries onto the counter.

"Hi, Elizabeth, I'm just-," I start explaining my lateness, but she frantically interrupts me.

"Blaire! It's your mom. She stopped breathing, and I had to call 911. I managed to get her heart going again before the emergency crew arrived, but her pulse is still very weak. They are rushing her to the ER."

Dropping the eggs in my hand, I race out of the store. Pushing aside people on the street, I run as fast as I can back to our apartment building. The siren wails in the distance when I go to turn the last corner. Elizabeth is waiting, wringing her hands while she paces the sidewalk.

Glancing in my direction, her face tells me everything I already know. My mom's time is quickly running out.

Chapter Five

Jaxxon

Raven. Since the night I watched her drive away, she is all I have thought about, morning, noon, and night. I think about her incredible body and the way she moved on that stage. I see her legs spread wide with her back arched, pleasuring herself. I envision her gagged and tied to my bed as I fuck her senseless with my cock. I can taste her on my tongue and feel her on my skin, even though I've yet to touch her. I've jerked off so many fucking times to this girl's memory that I've lost count. She is the only thing I want, the only thing I desire.

"JAXXON!" My father yells at me from across the conference table. I'm twenty-five-years old, and he makes me feel like I am five when he speaks my name like that.

Blinking out of my Raven trance, I focus in on his angry face. The other associates are exiting the room, and it is now just him and me. I know the meeting this morning had been important, but I can't get my mind in the game of anything except a stripper named Raven.

"May I remind you that we have a major meeting tomorrow with investors? If it fails, we risk losing patent on the new synthetic material for our new valve."

"I'm sorry, Father. I assure you I'm ready for the meeting," I lie. I am not ready for anything except tying up and fucking an ebony haired beauty.

“I suggest you get your head straight and in the game and prove to me that Ryder Technology is where you want to be. Just because you are my son, that doesn’t mean you are entitled to anything. Everyone earns his position here, and I am not about to hand the company off one day to a man who spends more time chasing ass than closing serious business deals.”

“Yes, Sir,” I reply, trying to suppress the anger and sarcasm in my voice. He is a fine one to be talking since I caught him fucking his assistant Chloe in his office yesterday.

I hate working with him, but I believe in what our company does. Things were great a few years ago when my Grandfather still ran the place. I learned so much from him and loved working by his side. Ever since he passed away last year, things have been extremely touchy with my dad.

Chloe interrupts us as she steps into the room. Her short, nothing there attire flatters her toned body, but her attractive face is cold and callous, just like my father. They honestly make the perfect pair. Smiling, my father stands and adjusts his pants. It doesn’t take a genius to know exactly what is about to happen. My hypocrite of a father is about to fuck his assistant on the conference room table the minute I leave.

“Jaxxon, will you excuse us? Chloe has some important papers I need to sign.”

“Yeah, whatever.” I snarl and stand to leave.

No sooner that the door closes behind me, I hear the familiar sound of the lock clicking. Rolling my eyes, I make my way down the hall to my office. Even though I hate to admit it, my father is right about me needing to be ready for tomorrow’s meeting. The patent we are trying to gain will save millions of lives. I need to do my part to make Grandfather proud. Taking my jacket off, I roll up my sleeves and walk over to close my office door. For the rest of the afternoon, I struggle to forget Raven and concentrate on finishing my presentation.

By the time I am satisfied, it is late, and everyone has been gone from the building for hours. Grabbing my jacket and keys, I make my way down to the parking garage and into my black Ferrari F12 Berlinetta. As I drive, every girl I pass on the side of the street is Raven. I honestly think I am going to go insane. Forcing myself to keep driving, I am almost to the turnoff to my apartment when I feel the overwhelming need to turn around and head back to Club Climax.

What the fuck? I am losing my shit over a fucking girl! No girl rules my life!

By the time I pull into the parking lot, I am worked up in desperation for her. When I enter the club, I'm once again welcomed by the girls that work there. Their hands slide down my chest as I walk past them, moving closer to the stage. Honey glances in my direction and then angrily looks away.

Yeah, it's safe to say she isn't going to be asking me for anything again.

I sit next to a group of drunken men who are waving dollar bills and shouting nasty comments at the girl working the pole. She is very attractive, and definitely a girl that would normally be satisfying to fill my hefty sexual appetite, but she doesn't hold a candle to the dark hair angel in my head.

Patiently, I sit and wait, pushing off the girls who try to sit in my lap or invite me into Ultimate Climax. I just want to see my girl perform. I need to fill this desire inside me.

After watching five more girls dance, I wave the heavy bouncer over to ask him when Raven is coming on.

"She didn't come in tonight."

"Is she working tomorrow night?" I ask him, not knowing if I can wait that long.

"Can't say. These girls here all have a mind of their own. They only work when they want to."

Handing him a hundred dollar bill, I give him a card with a message written on back.

"There's five hundred more for you if you make sure she gets this."

“Yes, Sir! I definitely will make sure she gets it.” He tucks the card into his leather vest pocket.

Tossing my whiskey back, I throw a twenty on stage for the girl dancing and then leave. It would be so easy finding a girl to agree to be tied up and fucked tonight, but I could come a thousand times, and never be satisfied until my seed coats the inside of my beautiful Raven.

As I close the door to my car, her memory flashes over me. My cock begs for release. Unzipping my jeans, I close my eyes, and she is there once more. Her fingers thrust inside of her, her face overcome with the pleasure she’s giving herself. I hear her moans; I hear her begging. Pumping my shaft and squeezing my balls, the stream of hot semen shoots up my abdomen. “Fuck!” I roar slamming my head back against my seat.

Catching a glance at myself in my rear view mirror, I don’t even recognize who that man is anymore. I have to get a grip on this situation and fast. No woman will ever have control over me; I am the one calling the shots. Raven will one day belong to me. Hopefully when she reads that card, she will agree to be just that.

Mine.

Blaire

I watch my mother through the ICU unit window. The doctor has been talking to me for at least a few minutes now, but I haven’t heard a damn word he has said. All I can think about is my mother laying in that room, hooked up to more machines than I can count, just in order for her to stay alive. I can’t even make out her face because of the large breathing tube that is connected to her mouth.

“Blaire? Blaire!” Dr. Landers yells my name and startles me out of my thoughts.

Blinking back to him, I see the look of sympathy on his face. I don’t want that look from him. I don’t want him telling me that she is dying. I already know that.

"Blaire, did you hear anything I just said?" he asks me.

"No, I'm sorry, Doctor Landers, I didn't. I just can't believe she is in there," I say motioning back to the room.

"I know that, my dear girl, but we've known this has been coming for a long time now. I had hoped we could hold off for a little while longer, but your mother has just reached a point where we can no longer wait. She needs to be on Dr. Flannery's trial program. He is the only doctor in this hospital that can perform that surgery successfully."

Hanging my head, I know that is impossible. Dr. Flannery is one of the world's leading heart surgeons, but he also comes with an enormously high price tag. He'd laugh his head off at my measly two thousand dollars that I had managed to save.

Oh God! What am I going to do?

"I know it is about the money, Blaire, and if it were up to me, I'd waive the fee, but this is different. Is there anyone at all that you can speak to that might be able to help you get the money you need?"

I don't have to think or hesitate to answer him. It is a simple response of shaking my head.

We have no one.

Putting his hand on my shoulder, he looks at me with remorse in his eyes. To me, this look is worse than sympathy. It means there is no hope, and I can't give up that easily; I wasn't raised that way. As Dr. Landers walks away, I feel the pain rise in my chest. I can't lose her.

There has got to be a way.

Reluctantly, I leave the hospital, heading back to the club. I have to go see Mike and let him know what is going on, so he doesn't fire me for not showing up at work last night. I'm also hoping he will front me my money from last week.

Glancing at the clock in my old Camry, I see that it is almost four o'clock in the afternoon. Club Climax should be opening up just about now and hopefully Mike is there. I park on the employee side and use my key to get in the back door. A few of the older girls that perform early are already in the dressing room getting ready. I ask Star where Mike is, and she informs me that he is in his office, talking to a couple of guys that work here.

Standing outside his office, I wait in the hallway to talk to him. Mike sees me and motions me inside. The moment I step in, I flash back to seeing Honey on her knees sucking off Beautiful Man. I struggle to pull my eyes away from the floor and walk further inside.

"Raven, are you alright?" he asks, taking in my appearance. Glancing down, I remember that I'd come straight from the hospital and I'd been up all night. I am sure I look like a hot mess.

"No. I've been at the hospital all night with my mom. She had a heart attack last night and isn't doing very well."

"I'm sorry to hear that." He motions for the men to leave.

"Do you know when you will be back to work?"

"I will do my best to be here tomorrow night. Because of expenses, I need to work as much as I can. Is there any way I can ask for an advance on my check for this past week?"

Mike nods his head and immediately begins opening his side drawer. Taking out a moneybag, he counts out a thousand dollars and hands it to me.

"But Mike, that is way more than what I made."

"Don't argue with me girl, just take it. I know you need it."

I feel horribly taking it, but shamefully I reach over and take it off the desk. I can't let my pride stand in the way of helping my mom. If I have to, I'll beg all over town, in order to get the money I need.

"Thank you so much, Mike. I'll work extra hours and pay you back," I promise him.

"You've brought me a lot of business since you started working here, Raven. Just consider it a 'thank you' bonus."

Standing, I thank him again before turning to leave. When I

walk out the door, I immediately slam into Big Jack's broad chest. The revolting combination of his bad breath, cigarettes, and strong cologne is enough to make me gag.

"Hey there, little girl, I got something for you." He says digging into the inside pocket of his leather jacket to retrieve it.

This is actually a little frightening because I can't imagine what he possibly could have for me.

"A guy came in the club last night looking for you. He said to make sure you got this," he informs before handing me a card. The minute I see the club card, I know exactly whom it's from.

"Thank you Big Jack," I say dismissing the card and discarding it into my coat pocket.

"Aren't you even going to look at it?" he asks me curiously.

"No, it is just some guy wanting me to go into Ultimate Climax with him. I'm not interested. I don't know why he just doesn't take one of the other girls."

"Well, you might want to take another look at that, Sweetheart. It might just change your mind." He says to me before walking off.

Curious as to what he said, I reach in my pocket to pull out the card, but suddenly my phone starts vibrating in my pocket. As I glance down at the screen, I see that it is the hospital calling. Holding my breath, I nervously answer it.

Please, Lord, don't let her be gone.

"Hello?"

"Ms. Michaels?" a lady's voice questions.

"Yes, this is she," I reply, terrified by what is coming next.

"Dr. Landers requested that you return to the hospital as quickly as possible."

"My mother… is she alright?" I ask as I run toward the back exit door.

"I'm afraid I am not at liberty to discuss anything else," she replies, and I end the call.

Panicked, I don't even bother buckling my seatbelt as I toss the phone in the seat beside me and spin out of the parking lot.

Once the elevator reaches the cardiac ICU floor, I run like a crazy person to my mother's room.

Dr. Landers stands there in front of my mother's unit with two other men. My body instantly halts and paralyzes me where I'm standing. His face is solemn and serious.

Oh God, No! She can't be gone! She can't be!

I fight to put one foot in front of the other to move ahead to him, but I can't. I know when I get there what he is going to say, and all I want to do is turn and run. Glancing in my direction, he nudges the man beside him.

When he motions me to join them, I force myself to move forward.

One foot in front of the other, Blaire. You can do this; you have to be strong.

"Blaire, this is Dr. Flannery and Dr. Conway. I was just discussing your mother's condition with them."

I turn around, look into the window of my mother's unit, and then look back at the men.

"So my mom is alright? I was worried from the call that she-" I can't even finish my sentence before tears spill down my face.

"Yes my dear, right now her condition is still the same. Dr. Flannery and I were just discussing her options." Nodding, I then turn my head towards Dr. Flannery.

"Ms. Michaels, I don't believe in beating around the bush or giving false hope to patients or their families, so I will be blunt. If your mother doesn't have surgery to correct her valve issue immediately, she won't live ten minutes once those machines are turned off," he says coldly while pointing at the room behind me. I turn and face the window and see my mother lying there helpless. This is the worst possible feeling anyone can ever have. To know that you would do anything for someone you love, yet the anything in this case would never be enough.

Shoving my hands into my pocket, I feel the sharp edge of the glossy card as it rakes across my fingertip. Slowly, I ease it out and read the words on the back.

Raven,

Ultimate Climax

You name the price.

Mr. R

834-9239

Closing my eyes, I gather my courage and then look back at my mother. I had meant what I had said earlier to myself. I will do anything for her, even if it is taking everything from me at the same time. Turning back to face Dr. Flannery, I look blankly into his eyes.

"Schedule the surgery, Dr. Flannery," I reply while gripping the card tightly in my hand, and placing it back into my coat pocket.

"I am not a charity case, Ms. Michaels. I can't afford to be in this business," he snaps back, and I see Dr. Landers grow angry.

"Richard! That isn't necessary!" Dr. Landers shoots at Dr. Flannery.

Holding my hand up, I walk toward the arrogant bastard that deems himself as "GOD" and point my finger into his chest.

"Just schedule the surgery. The money will be there!" I blast angrily and then turn to walk back down the hall, darting into the first ladies room I see.

Closing the door, I'm relieved to see I am alone. Securing the lock on the door, I reach back into my pocket to retrieve the card.

Can I really do this?

You don't have a choice. The voices in my head continue battling against one another.

Wringing my hands, I manage to dial the number on the card. As it rings, I can feel Raven take over for me. She has to, because Blaire can't do this.

Chapter Six

Jaxxon

The meeting with our investors went extraordinarily well. Thanks to my presentation, Ryder Technology managed to secure the investors needed to gain the patent for the new synthetic material to use for the latest heart valve we have designed. The conference room is loud and full of excitement as people move to congratulate my father and me on landing the deal. Funny thing is that, as I stand beside my father, I realize he is the only person in this room I want to praise me. I know it will be a cold day in Hell before that ever happens.

Stacy, from accounting, has had one too many glasses of champagne and is now whispering into my ear. Even though we've fucked a few times in the past, I've never done any of the heavy stuff with her; I can't risk that kind of thing getting out here at work.

"Let's get out of here," she whispers in my ear.

I won't lie; the temptation is definitely there.

But why is it temptation?

It should be so easy to pull her into the back office or into the bathroom and bend her over, yet it's not. As my hand slides down her waist, my mind flashes to the dark haired beauty that haunts me at every chance.

"Not tonight," I reply, walking away to get a drink. I don't have to turn around to see the daggers that she shooting with her eyes into my back. The sudden buzzing in my pocket startles me and sends me jumping, just as I am lifting the glass of champagne to my lips, causing it to spill onto my suit.

"Fuck!" I say while digging out my phone. Angrily, I answer it without even looking to see whom it is calling.

"What?" I scream into the phone while patting my jacket with a napkin I grabbed off the nearby server's tray. My anger serves them right for causing me to ruin a thousand dollar suit jacket.

"Um, Mr. R?" Her smooth quiet voice fills my ears and I know instantly whom it belongs to.

Raven.

"Yes, just a moment," I manage to say, covering the speaker while making my way to a quieter place to talk. I thought I was prepared for this call; however, I'm not. When I reach a quieter office, I hesitate a few moments before speaking back to her. I can hear the nervousness in her breathing and it drives me insane with desire. Adjusting the erection in my pants, I finally begin speaking.

"Alright, continue," I reply, asserting authority in my tone.

"This is Raven. I am calling you to discuss your offer for Ultimate Climax."

Her words are like music to my ears and, of course, to my dick. I am willing to pay her a very obscene amount of money to have complete and utter control of her fucking hot ass body.

"Very well, we will meet tonight to discuss our arrangement. I expect you to be in front of the club by 7 pm."

"I will be there, Mr. R."

My cock throbs at the way she says my name. The moment we end our call, I miss her voice. Looking at the time, I see that I need to get moving in order to prepare for meeting her. Tonight, no matter what the cost, Raven will be mine.

Chapter Seven

Blaire

I should be getting ready right now for tonight, but instead, I am standing over my mother's hospital bed holding her frail hand in mine. The machines around her steadily beep while the vent in her mouth continues to push air into her lungs every so many seconds. I watch her chest rise and fall, and listen to the loud beeping of her pulse echo through the room. For now, these things comfort me. They are proof she is still here with me.

Since there is so much preparation required before surgery, Dr. Flannery can't schedule it until the beginning of next week. To be perfectly honest, I am terrified, but I'm also relieved at the same time. Even if he is not my favorite person right now, he is the only hope I have of keeping her alive. I know this is her only chance at resuming a normal life; I just pray she gets that chance.

I know that I don't have much time, so I gently lay her hand that I am holding back by her side. Stroking her hair once more, I assure myself that what I am about to do is the right thing.

"I love you, Mom."

Quickly, I place a kiss on her forehead and exit the room. If I get to the club soon, I might have time to grab a shower there before having to meet with this Mr. R.

Traffic is crazy this time of day, but I manage to arrive in time to prepare there. Stepping into the hot shower, I take my time preparing every area of my body for tonight. I know that usually the Ultimate Climax room stays busy, so hopefully it will be occupied and I will have to do this another night.

I mean a girl can hope, can't she?

Saying that I am nervous would the understatement of the year. I coach myself the entire time I smooth lotion onto my skin. This meeting has to go well, especially now that I have too much at stake. Since I didn't have time to go home first for my normal clothes, I select one of my favorite short black skirts, pairing it along with a vibrant red zip up jacket. I finish off my ensemble with my tall black stiletto boots that lace almost all the way up to my knee. I am sure this outfit screams hooker, but it is the only suitable thing I can come up with in my wardrobe that I keep here.

I have a few minutes before I have to be out front, so I decide to take the opportunity and duck my head into Mike's office to let him know that I will be back at work tomorrow night. He nods his head and writes me down on the schedule in front of him. Closing his door behind me, I take a deep breath and make my way outside to wait as instructed.

Promptly at seven o'clock on the dot, a sleek new black Range Rover pulls up to the front entrance and stops. A short stocky guy steps out of the vehicle and smiles widely at me. Instantly, I try to hide my displeasure as I look him over. He is at least fifty years old with a decent size gut. This guy doesn't look like he had sounded on the phone, but I guess no one ever does. The thought of him touching me makes me sick at my stomach. I can feel the bile rising in the back of my throat.

The moment he speaks, I am relieved.

"Ms. Raven?" he says, and I immediately know this is not the seductive, deep voice that I heard on the phone earlier.

I nod my head at him and force a smile back.

"I've been instructed to drive you to your designated meeting."

Opening the back door of the SUV, he extends his hand to help me climb into the tan leather seat.

Once inside, I spot a black silk scarf in the seat next to me. Picking it up, I turn back looking confused at the man who is still holding the door open.

"I must insist that you place this on before we leave. I've been instructed to inform you that if you remove the blindfold that the deal is off. Is that understood?" He warns me. I try to compose the fear rising in my chest.

Why the blindfold? This can't be good. I'm going with a complete stranger to meet another complete stranger. No one even knows where I am, or where I am going. *What the hell am I doing? Don't be stupid, Blaire. GET OUT!*

"The blindfold, Ms. Raven," the man's voice pulls me out of my trance and back into making my terrifying choice. Nodding at him, I hesitantly secure the material around my face. He leans in and checks it before closing my door. Another door opens and shuts and soon we are leaving the parking lot.

We make several turns before we finally come to a stop. The back door opens and I feel a hand take mine to help me out of the vehicle.

We pause for a moment before I am placed into another car. I feel the cool leather underneath my skin and then I hear the door shut beside of me. Instantly, I sense that I am not alone in this car. Terror evokes me. I fight the urge to not remove the blindfold.

"Hello, Raven." His voice rolls over me like warm silk.

"Hello," I reply, unsure of what to say to him next.

"I am sorry to have to blindfold you, but a man in my position requires complete discretion. I appreciate that you respected my wishes," he says while touching the fabric on the side of my face. As affectionate as it had felt, I know he is also checking the tightness of the fabric. My skin still tingles at where he'd touched me.

"I admit that it bothers me, but I understand your reasons," I explain.

"Very good. Let's get down to business then, shall we?" he asks, and I study his voice carefully. He sounds young, perhaps even near my age. I wonder how far off I am in my prediction.

"Yes."

"Now that you have had time to consider my offer, may I ask the amount of money you are requiring for our arrangement?" He asks very coyly. I swallow the lump in my throat and take a deep breath. Hopefully, when I give him the figure I need, he won't tell me no.

"Forty thousand dollars." I manage to say while barely controlling the shaking in my voice. Although he had said on the card to name the price, forty thousand dollars is a far cry from his original five thousand dollar offer.

What if he refuses to pay that amount? What will I do then?

Oh, shit! He is quiet. *Way* too quiet.

I hear the clink of ice hitting the glass and then the liquid being poured inside. He takes a deep breath before continuing, "I see. So forty thousand dollars for one night, is that correct?"

"Yes." I answer him while holding my breath.

"May I ask what changed your mind?"

I struggle to decide what to say in response.

"I just need the money."

"Forty thousand dollars is a lot of money, Raven."

"Yes, Sir. I understand that."

"I see. Well, what if I were to tell you that I have another proposition for you?"

"Another proposition? I'm afraid I don't understand what you are saying."

He takes a deep breath and leans forward, taking my hands into his. Slowly, he caresses the skin around my wrists and lifts them up to his lips. The fear I once had been feeling now evaporates. The thing is, I should be terrified right now, but instead, for some reason, something in his voice that soothes me. I shouldn't be attracted to this at all. I feel like a stupid girl who has opened herself up into a world that she has never known.

"My offer to you is a contract of sorts. I will, of course, agree to your fee and have it wired to you, but only after the contract is complete."

"A contract? I'm sorry, but I'm not following you. I thought we were agreeing to just one night."

"I am most certain now that one night will not be enough with you, Sweetheart. I wish to extend this relationship a bit further with at least the promise of a two-week agreement. After which, you will be released from your obligation. I am afraid for the kind of money you are asking, I will have to insist on this being under my terms."

"What will this contract involve?"

"It is quite simple. By agreeing, you will be my submissive for the next fourteen days. You will be exclusively mine. If that is a problem for a boyfriend or husband, then I'm afraid we will have a problem."

"I am single. Not many girls like me are in relationships."

"Very good. I can't tell you how much that pleases me to hear that, Raven."

"You will available to me at all times. I will provide a phone for you and you are to keep it with you, no exceptions. Failure to answer will immediately violate our agreement. I do not make calls twice. When I tell you to do something, you are not to challenge me in any way. For the next two weeks, you will be mine, Raven, in every possible way. Are you willing to accept my offer?"

My chest burns with each intake of air. I don't know what to do or what to say. If I say no to him, then I will lose the money and will be forced to cancel my mother's surgery. There is no way I can do that. If I say yes, then that means two whole weeks of allowing my body to be used and controlled by a complete stranger. If I say yes, I will become a whore.

Why has my life come down to this?

I am basically trading my soul to the devil himself, in order to save my mother.

“Well, Raven? I need an answer. I am not a patient man and I have needs. What is it going to be?”

“If I say yes, is there any way I can get the money upfront?”

“Why is it so important for you to have the money now?”

“I-it’s an emergency.” I stammer. I don’t want him to know. I don’t want him to feel pity for me.

“A forty thousand dollar emergency? So what is it? If you don’t get the money then someone dies or something?” he jokes, but I don’t laugh. He is joking, but he has no idea just how true his words actually are. I’m glad the blindfold hides the tears that are forming in my eyes.

“Yes. Actually it is a matter of life and death.” I reply but he remains silent. I take a deep breath and gather all the courage I have inside of me. I have so much to lose in what I am about to say, but I have to call his bluff.

“I’m afraid that as much as I need the money, if you can’t provide the transaction up front, I’ll be unable to agree to anything.”

Silence again fills the car. I hear the clinking of the ice in the drink and hear him exhale. Suddenly, his hand is on my thigh, and I feel the energy surge through my core. Something about him is so unbelievably powerful and attractive. I only wish I could see him. I feel his breath on my mouth as he moves closer to me. His finger skims my lips slowly, causing me to tremble.

“I’ll agree to front you the money, Raven, but only under one condition.”

“What?” I stammer.

“I have already secured Ultimate Climax. We must begin tonight. Do we have a deal?”

Swallowing my fear, I give him my answer.

"Yes."

Jaxxon

She has no idea how unbelievably sexy she looks right now sitting across from me blindfolded. Once I had laid eyes on her, I couldn't help myself. I had to reach across and touch her. One touch of her skin leaves my body radiating with electrified energy that I'd never before experienced with anyone.

I zone in on her delicious mouth as she speaks. Those plump glossy cherry red lips of hers beg to be kissed. I can't wait to see them wrapped around my cock as I fuck her mouth relentlessly. Her short as fuck skirt shows off her long toned legs. And God help me, those boots are killing me! As I sit here, trying to listen to her, my mind and body are elsewhere thinking of things to do to her. When it comes time to discuss a figure for her services, I prepare myself for a high amount, but no matter the price, I will pay.

Even though I had prepared to pay a much higher figure than forty thousand dollars, I use the opportunity to seal the deal on contracting her as my submissive. I need this now more than ever in my life, and I most definitely need it with her. I've never felt such extreme desire. I've never had such ravenous thoughts before. One time with her will not possibly be enough to get her out of my system. Honestly, when it comes to her, I don't know if there are enough times.

The only thing is, I can't figure out is why she's agreeing to all of this now, especially at such a high price tag. I can't understand how anyone could need that kind of money without it involving drugs or something illegal. Even though she doesn't look like a drug addict, she is, however, a stripper. I am sure her world is full of making bad choices. When I make a joke about it being life or death, she doesn't laugh. I guess this deal is more serious than I had thought. When she'd turned the tables on me and threatened to walk away if I didn't give her the money first, I heard the demon in me scream. How dare she try to take control of this so soon? I will definitely need to show her who is in charge here.

Once we reach an agreement, I make it known that I do not intend on wasting any time. I want her in that room tonight. I plan on fucking her in every way possible, hard and rough, until I can no longer stand. With my stamina, that should be a very, very long time.

Ultimate Climax is normally a busy room at Club Climax, but after paying a hefty price tag, I'd managed to secure it all night long from the owner of the club. I don't want to be rushed when it comes to the things I have in store for this girl. I will have her so broken in and addicted to me that by the time the contract is up, she won't ever want to leave. I am pretty sure by that time I'll have fucked her out of my system. At least that is what I hope to be the case.

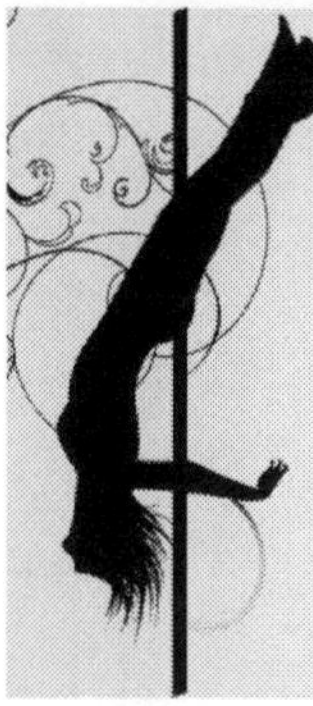

Chapter Eight

Blaire

My heart is pounding so hard right now that I'm convinced it's going to leap out of my chest. Beads of sweat form on my forehead as I struggle to breathe steadily. I reach and grab a hold of the bronze handle of the door and hesitate a moment before opening it. I know that once I walk through this door, there is no going back. I know once I do, my life will never be the same.

You don't have a choice, Blaire. You have to do this. You need the money.

I walk in and close the heavy wooden door behind me. Even though I've been working all these months here, this is the first time I have been brave enough to venture inside. I've heard plenty of stories from girls who frequent Ultimate Climax. Most tales of bondage would frighten the hell out of a virgin, but for some reason I find them erotic. I just never thought I'd be losing my virginity and introduced to this lifestyle, all at the same time.

Glancing around, I slowly take in every detail of the large room before me. It is decorated in warm rich colors of deep reds and purple. The black textured walls are accented by the dark glossy wooden floor. The long wall to the left has a built in case that houses whips and belts, along with long canes and leather sticks that I think are called crops. Handcuffs, restraints, and ropes all in various sizes, dangle from metal hooks on the shelves. The light from the enclosed compartment dances off the beautiful glass dildos that are on display inside the curio. I stop and marvel at their spiral shape and length; I can't help but imagine that as being painful. Silently, I pray that he doesn't choose to use one of those on me.

Curiously, I walk closer and open each of the long drawers underneath the display case. Each drawer is filled with everything from lubrication, anal plugs, gags, other sex toys, to what I assume to be nipple clamps. Every item is sealed in plastic, varying in shapes, colors, and sizes.

Will he use these on me?

My face blushing from embarrassment, I shove the last drawer, close it, and quickly back away.

What the fuck have I gotten myself into? I am about to have sex with a complete stranger for money. I am nothing but a dirty whore.

I need the money, but what will this guy do once he realizes that I've never had sex before, let alone done anything like this?

Will he be revolted and throw me out?

I can't risk losing this offer; my mom's operation comes first. I can't tell him now, because then he may not want me. I will just have to remain quiet and bite through the pain. I just hope he doesn't notice that I'm still a virgin.

Who am I kidding? Of course, he is going to notice!

Like a magnetic pull, I am instantly drawn to the enormous four-poster bed in the middle of the room. White sheer fabric flows at each side of the attached canopy that is attached overhead. It makes the scene around me look almost sweet and romantic. (That is, of course, if you consider the adjustable iron shackles that are attached at both the head and foot of the bed to be romantic). The wooden headboard is beautifully carved with intricate designs of angels and demons. Lightly tracing the wood with my fingertips, I assume this is someone's version of Heaven and Hell. Perhaps it is a warning to me of the path, of which, I am about to choose.

Walking around the bed, my eyes instantly spot the white box sitting on top of the deep purple chaise lounge. Moving closer, I see a tag with my name written on it. Laying the card aside, I gently lift the top of the box up and dare a glance inside. A beautiful silk woven piece of fabric lays inside along with instructions.

Pulling the silk out of the box, I revel in how soft it is upon my skin. I hold the note up and begin reading.

Shoes and panties only. Put on blindfold and get on the chair on your hands and knees. You are not to move or speak until instructed to do so. Harsh punishment will be given for disobedience. Remember, Raven, I am in complete control. Behind these doors, you follow my rules.

You have three minutes.

What? Who is this guy?

I stand frozen, staring down at the written commands in front of me.

Can I really do this?

Suddenly, a powerful voice echoes through the speakers of the dimly lit room.

"Two minutes. Move!"

"Jesus!" I scream, almost jumping out of my skin.

"You are disappointing me, Raven. I assure you that's not something you want to do!"

His demands fill my body with erotic fear. Something about his voice is so unbelievably intoxicating. Now that I am aware he can see me, I grow even more timid and nervous. I freely take my clothes off for the strange men outside on that stage, but undressing in front of him seems so much more intimate and personal. I think of my mother and how frail and weak she looked on my visit earlier with her. I can't lose her. I'd rather lose myself this way. Closing my eyes, I do it. I turn the switch and leave Blaire behind. When my eyes reopen, I become Raven.

I pull on the sash of my black silk robe and allow it to fall to the floor behind me. Slowly, I inch my arms around to my back and unclasp the bra that I am wearing. My tits fall freely out of the black lace as I drop the garment beside the robe. I feel so exposed and dirty in a way that I've never felt before. Embarrassed, I cover my chest with my free hand and ease myself onto the lounger to sit. Taking one last look around at the room, I eye the door on the back wall. It's so well camouflaged to look like the wall that it's no wonder I missed it when I first walked in. This must be where he will enter the room.

I hear the doorknob turn, and I panic. Frantically, I tie the fabric around my eyes and get on all fours. The door shuts behind me and I hear footsteps inching closer to me. SHIT! My heart is pounding faster and harder than it ever has before. Oh God! I feel like I am going to pass out.

Being blindfolded heightens and intensifies every one of my senses. I zone in on the sounds of the room. His loud footsteps echo loudly around me. At first, I can tell that he is getting closer, but then suddenly the footsteps stop, and I can no longer hear anything at all. The deafening silence is killing me. I turn my head to the side trying to listen, but still there is nothing. I know he is in the room because I can feel the powerful energy around me.

Taking two steps closer, he stops behind me, and I hold my breath. Without warning, a violent sting erupts across my exposed backside as his hand makes contact with my flesh.

"I warned you to be ready. You will not disobey me!"

The pain is so intense that it causes my eyes to water. Holding in my screams, I bite down hard into my lip and immediately I taste the metallic flavor of my own blood.

"I can't do this! You have to!" The voices in my head continue to battle with one another. I want to scream, but it won't do me any good. This room is completely soundproof. Screams are a part of what goes on in here. Even if they could hear me, no one would come into this room

Music begins to play loudly around me. I recognize Kings of Leon's "Closer" as it bellows out of the speakers.

I feel his fingertip lightly trace over my face. His touch ignites every nerve ending in my body, causing me to begin trembling on the chair. The fact I can't see what is happening is scary as fucking hell, but it's also turning me on in ways my body has never known. I feel his breath as he inches his mouth closer to mine. Each heated breath against me makes my sex throb harder and harder.

Oh God!

Forcefully, he grabs my jaw and squeezes the skin hard, yanking me closer toward him. His mouth is inches from mine. The beautiful man that I can't seem to stop thinking about invades my mind. I want this to be him touching me instead of some stranger that I'm not even allowed to see. With the eluded fantasy in my head, I lean more into him, anticipating him to kiss me, but he doesn't. I feel the warm blood begin to trickle down my lip and suddenly his hot tongue is there, gently swiping it away.

Holy fuck that is hot!

"You are so beautiful, Raven," he whispers into my ear before taking my lobe in with his teeth. Unconsciously, I slacken my posture and shift my weight forward, losing myself in the feel of his touch.

"I said don't move!"

Two hard smacks are suddenly given to my sore ass and this time my sex squeezes, drenching my panties with my intense pleasure. I never imagined it would feel so good to be punished, but the idea of what else he could do terrifies me. I don't want to displease him.

Why is that?

"I see that you are a rule breaker. That displeases me very much, I'm afraid. I chose to go easy on you the first time, but trust me, there will be nothing easy about the next time. I don't tolerate people disrespecting me, Raven."

"I have admired you for quite some time. I am glad you finally agreed to my offer," he says wrapping my long hair around his hand. He jerks my head back, lifting my face to his and speaks against my lips.

"We have some things to discuss. Understand this! When we

are behind these doors, you are mine completely. Nod if you understand." He orders and I nod back at him.

"You will not speak at all, unless I give you permission and you are to address me as "Sir" every time you do. You will not touch yourself or come unless I tell you that you can," he orders while he slides his hand in between my thighs.

"And most importantly, you will not remove that blindfold for any reason what so ever."

I am afraid to speak or move. What do I do? I'll tell you what I do. I don't answer him.

"Answer me!" he roars angrily slapping my tits hard with his hand. I catch myself before I fall forward.

"Yes, Sir." I manage to answer him through the pain radiating through my nipples.

"Excellent! Very good, Sweetheart," he says, dragging his lips across my cheek. His breath smells of delicious iced cinnamon; his body smells of a rich heavy spice. One I gladly would love to get lost in.

Suddenly, a soft silk piece of fabric is slowly dragged across my face and placed around my mouth.

"Open and bite down," he orders me and I immediately comply. He secures the fabric into my mouth and then kisses my lips. I hear his footsteps on the wood floor again as he goes to move behind me.

His hand tenderly caresses the spot where he'd spanked me earlier. I hear his breathing increase with each stroke to my ass. The gentleness is fast replaced with roughness when he sinks his nails into my flesh. Dragging them slowly to the side, he stops and laughs before releasing them. I feel both of his hands tightly grip hold of my hips. Suddenly, the lace string on both sides of my ass digs deep into my flesh. It's so violent and rough that I swear he's going to bruise or tear my skin in the process. The small lace patch pulls at my sex. It causes me to whimper, but I manage to muffle it.

I want more of this. What is wrong with me?

I hear him laughing at my desperation. He tightens his hold again and pulls upward on the strings, forcing my ass up high into the air.

"Mmmm. I can smell that delicious cunt, Baby. I want to taste it," he hisses through his teeth. Furiously, he flips me onto my back, causing the wind to be knocked from my chest.

"Spread these fucking legs for me! Now!" he demands.

I don't have a chance to move before his hands grip both my thighs and vigorously forces them open. His nose slowly trails across my sex. He releases a loud groan, causing me to tremble with immense pleasure.

"Remember, you are not to come until I tell you to. Is that understood? Nod your head yes or no."

Quickly, I nod in response to him. He inhales my essence again before diving back into my crevices. Each additional release of hot air against my sex leaves me gasping and craving for more.

How can I feel this way? He is a complete stranger and I am about to have sex with him. What is wrong with me?

He runs his nose up my folds and bites at the fabric, taking part of my clit with him. I try to hold in the moan, but it escapes my lips. With one giant yank, I hear the rip of my panties and feel his tongue plunge deep inside of me.

Oh God!

His grip tightens on my bottom as he continues assaulting my sex with his tongue. Deeper and deeper, the strokes of his hot tongue spiral me into a blissful Heaven.

He grabs my ass to keep me close to him, and quickly, I find myself rocking my hips against his mouth. Before I can blink, I feel it building inside me, deep and low. I may be a virgin, but I definitely know what an orgasm is. I've managed to pull some pretty damn good ones off before on my own, but nothing can compare to this. He flickers his tongue and then lifts up on my clit with his finger massaging it in a circular motion. Faster and faster he moves. The sensation is so incredible that I can feel tears forming in my eyes. I've never felt anything this good before. Knowing that I'm not allowed to come has me sweating and silently pleading in desperation. The feeling continues to grow and intensify until I don't think I can hold it in much longer without exploding. I bite deep onto the silk cloth in my mouth and suppress the scream inside of me.

"Come for me, Raven. Come now!" He commands, slapping my clit hard with his hand.

He drags his tongue up and then shoves his fingers deep inside me over and over.

I throw my head back and scream through the gag.

I can feel the warm release of my pussy juices and hear him growl in appreciation. The warmth of his face returns between my legs as he feverishly licks and sucks, cleaning all of my release from me.

"You are so fucking delicious, but I already knew that sweet cunt of yours would be, Baby."

My head is spinning so much from the intense orgasm, and for a brief moment, I swear I forget my own name. Rolling my eyes back in my head, I relish in the blissful high he's given me. Completely sated, I start slouching forward, but then he grabs a hold of my long hair again and pulls back hard on my head.

"I said don't fucking move! I am not done with you yet!" his powerful voice shouts.

My arms are suddenly grabbed and I am pulled off of where I'm lying. Stumbling over my feet, I try the best I can to follow him as he blindly leads me. He abruptly stops. Gently, I am being lifted up in his arms and cradled against his strong chest. I place my hand on his hot skin just above his heart. I can feel it beating hard and fast against my palm. Falling back, I feel the coolness of the satin sheets beneath me.

I am on the bed. Breathe, Blaire.

"You like doing this to me, don't you, Raven? I think you like being a bad girl. Feel what you are doing to me," he says while placing his hard, long cock in my hands. Unconsciously, I grab and pull down on his shaft.

Where did that come from?

My hands are grabbed and the sound of metal moving causes me to jump. He pushes down on my wrists and forcefully closes what sounds like a shackle over each of them before repeating the same thing to my ankles. My legs are opened further and further. I now lay spread eagle, exposing every known part of me to this man.

Smooth flaps of a leathery material are drawn up my stomach causing me to squirm. It both tickles and turns me on at the same time.

Why is he being gentle with me now?

WHOP! WHOP! The leather straps now slap at my pussy. I throw my head back and bite down into the gag. I can't say that it hurts; it only makes my desire crazier. My pussy throbs for another release. The bed sinks beside me and then I feel him straddling me.

The gag is jerked free from my mouth. I feel his heat approach my mouth as his cock teases my lips. I have never done this before with a guy, so I'm clueless of what comes next.

"Open that hot mouth of yours and suck it hard!" he demands but fear overtakes me and I hesitate.

"I *said* open your fucking mouth!" he screams from above me.

I barely get it open before he is thrusting his cock inside. He hits my gag spot and slides back out quickly. Grabbing my face, he forcefully shoves my head up and down onto him.

"Suck!" he screams and I draw in my jaw tighter. My mouth milks him hard. "Fuck yes! Just like that." I can taste his delicious salty flavor of his skin on my tongue as he continues shoving himself harder and harder into my mouth.

"You have a dirty little mouth and I am going to fill it up. When I do, you are going to hold it all in that mouth. Don't you fucking dare swallow a drop until I say! I am going to claim your throat."

Fisting my hair in his hands, I am yanked up to match his thrusts. "FUCK YES! AGGHHH! I'm coming!" he screams and I feel the warm, salty thickness fill my mouth. I find the unique salty flavor delicious so I savor his cum in my mouth.

"Let me see. Open your mouth and show me how much of my seed you have in there. Don't let any leak out!"

Carefully, I move my lips to open up for him to show him how full he has filled me. My mouth so full I can feel some of it spill to the back of my throat.

"Fuck yes! Look at all that cum. This is me claiming another part of you," he says as he grabs my jaw and squeezes it tightly.

"Swallow it all now! Don't you even think about spitting it out!"

The thick consistency gags me at first, but I manage to get it all down in one giant gulp.

"Open!" he orders again, jerking my head up to inspect my now empty mouth.

"Yes that is it. Taste it, Baby. That is my seed floating around in your stomach."

When he releases my jaw, I drop my head and lick my lips. He takes a huge intake of breath before passionately crashing his mouth to mine. Our tongues massage the mixture of our flavors together and I find it erotic as hell.

Why am I enjoying this? He has me chained up and blindfolded. What am I becoming?

"Fucking hell your pussy is so damn beautiful. It's drenched and glistening just for me. I'm going to bury my cock deep into your cunt and fuck you senseless," he says, slapping my wet opening.

I hear the tear of what I'm guessing is a condom and then I feel him move in front of me on the bed. He begins pulling something and suddenly my legs are being hoisted up higher into the air. When my ankles are high above my head, I begin writhing on the bed. I feel like a pig that is about to get roasted above a fire.

My ass is smacked over and over again, causing me to throw my head back and hold in my pleasure.

"I'm going to fuck you now. That is what you want isn't it, Raven? I'm going to make you come so hard you're going to scream and beg for more, but you are not going to make a sound or come unless I tell you that you can." Moving closer to me, I feel him tease his cock against my soaking wet folds.

Here it goes; this is it.

I tense my body and he slaps my pussy with his hand. "Relax!" he orders.

He leans in between my legs and I feel him slowly push himself into my hot drenched opening.

"Fuck, Baby! Your pussy is so fucking tight and wet." He pushes halfway in and the pain hits me. Oh, God it hurts! I hold the whimper in; I can't let him know. One more thrust and he will break completely through the skin, taking my innocence along with it. He inches himself out and I begin bracing myself for the next twinge of pain. Instead, he stills and I hear his loud gasp erupt into the room.

"What the fuck?"

He leaps off the bed and I hear him begin cursing loudly in the background.

"GODDAMN IT!"

Confused of what is going on, I dare a chance and speak.

"What is wrong? Why are you stopping?" I ask but he doesn't answer me.

"Please. I can't lose this job; I need this money." I plead.

I hear his heavy footsteps across the wood floor and then my hands are grabbed. For a moment, I think he is going to punish me for speaking, but then I hear the metal click and feel my hands freed. Lowering my legs down, he unsnaps the clasps and frees me from the bed. I am too afraid to move.

“Get dressed! That is all!” I hear footsteps charge out of the room and the door slam behind it.

Jaxxon

She’s a virgin? This just can’t be happening right now. She’d been so fucking hot and tight, her sweet pussy dripping wet for me. But the moment I saw blood on the condom and felt her tense up, I knew she’d never had sex before. No matter how hard I try, I can’t seem to wrap my mind around this right now.

How can she strip for a fucking living and never have been with a guy before?

Fuck!

Pulling furiously at my hair, I glance over at the monitor that is still running in the room that I’m in. This room is set up just like my place in my apartment. There she sits trembling with her knees pulled in toward her chest. I watch her bring her shaking hands up above her head and touch the material around her face with her fingertips. She begins to untie the blindfold, but then suddenly, she stops and pulls her hands away. It’s as if she is unsure of what to do next. Her obedience to me both fascinates and raises my curiosity. Walking closer to the monitor, I witness her drop her head and cover her face with her hands. Her elegant shoulders begin shaking and I feel my stomach drop. I don’t understand any of this. Why is she crying? I’m the one who should be pissed right now.

With each shake of her delicate shoulders, my anger lifts and is replaced with guilt. I had almost taken her innocence from her and she was going to allow me to do it. Don’t get me wrong, I’ve slept with a lot of virgins, but that had been back when I was a teenager. Now days, it is almost unheard of for a girl to still be one at my age. If her virginity had been so damned important to her, then why is she willing to sell herself to me? What is so pressing that she would be willing to sell her innocence at a forty thousand dollar price tag? Trust me, I definitely will be finding an answer to that one!

Her muffled cries grow even louder through the monitor speaker, intensifying so much that it begins pounding in my ears. If it is one thing I can't stand, it's a woman crying! What the fuck does it accomplish anyways except show weakness? Lunging forward, I jerk the sound knob so hard that I nearly break it off. Even though now I can't hear anything, I can't bring myself to stop watching her on the screen either.

Damn it!

I should just walk the fuck away, but I can't.

God help me; I just can't.

I open up the door again as quietly as I possibly can. She is now rocking back and forth, crying uncontrollably, with her head tucked down into her knees. Inching closer to her, I make my way towards the bed, but then the wooden floor beneath me suddenly creaks, giving me away. Jolting upwards in panic, she begins pushing her way back to the headboard to sit up straight. She looks so goddamn beautiful right now that I can't stop myself. I've never felt this way before. It's as if my body is gravitating to her on its own will. I zone in on those delicious lips and with one final move, place my knee on the bed next to her. No words have yet been spoken, my lips only seeming to have one destination in mind.

"Shhhh! It's alright," I whisper against her mouth before dragging my lips against hers. I'm unsure of where this newfound compassion is coming from. I don't console; I don't have the patience for weak people.

The soaked blindfold can no longer hold her tears. Mesmerized, I watch closely as the liquid drips down her flawless cheek. Like a moth to a flame, I ease forward catching the stream of tears with the tip of my tongue. The instant I taste the salty flavor I can no longer hold back. Crashing my lips to hers, I gently slide my arm around her waist, pulling her down from the headboard. Our tongues move hungrily together, my mouth capturing her moans.

I want in her now!

Sliding my free hand down her sternum, I feel her delectable body relax to my touch.

Good girl.

Moving further down, I feel how soaked she still is from earlier. Pressing my thumb into her clit, I feverishly begin maneuvering it around in circles. Her body arches below me as she bites down hard again on her bottom lip to hold in her pleasure.

"Let go," I reply before easing two fingers inside of her.

Fucking Hell! Watching her come is one of the hottest things that I've ever seen!

Her teeth slide off her bottom lip and the most wonderful blissful scream erupts from her body as she comes hard on my hand. I lift up and unzip my pants, shoving my boxer briefs down with them. Retrieving another condom from my pants pocket, I waste no time rolling it on my starving cock.

I feel her body tense again as I move back in between her thighs. Lifting up her long leg, I tenderly caress her smooth silky skin all the way down to her hip. As I position myself at her glorious entry, I gaze down on her one last time before easing myself inside of her.

She is so fucking tight and wet that I don't think I am going to be able to last two seconds. Even though she is blindfolded, I can see her gorgeous face growing pained as I push on into her so I stop. Reaching down, I grab her face and whisper against her lips, "Ready?"

"Yes," she breathlessly answers me and I brush away her midnight curls away from her face. I want to see her when I claim her for the first time. The Dominant in me wants to look into her eyes, but I can't risk removing that blindfold from her. Not yet anyways.

Placing my hands beside her on the bed, I push hard and fast into her, breaking the skin and completely taking away the last of her innocence from her. She gasps at first, but quickly I pick up the pace and she begins moving along with me. Each time I pull out, her pussy clamps down around me and milks my dick, completely spiraling me out of control. I don't think I have ever felt anything so fucking incredible in all my life. Each tiny movement has me ready to explode all in her.

What is wrong with me? This never happens! I can fuck for hours without ever coming.

Her long legs grow tighter around my waist and I know if I don't change positions with her soon that I will be done before we barely get started. I don't ever want to be referred to as a minute man. Firmly I press down on her hips and roll to my back while lifting her on top allowing her to straddle me.

"Ride me," I instruct her but she freezes. I can tell she is nervous and unsure of what to do.

Grabbing her ass, I slowly lift her up and then ease her down onto me. Her sweet hot folds envelop my cock perfectly, making the heaviness in my balls to cause them to ache. Each movement inside of her body drives me insanely close to the edge.

Christ! I'm not going to make it this way for long either! What is she doing to me?

A few more times of guiding her and she's gotten the hang of things quite well.

Oh Dear God, has she ever gotten the hang of things!

She places her soft hands on my chest and arches her back as she slowly rides me up and down. I lift my ass upwards meeting each and every thrust in perfect sync with her. Her long onyx waves bounce around her shoulders exposing her glorious tits to me. I'm rendered powerless the moment I gaze up at the goddess above me. Suddenly her nails dig into my chest and I wrap my arms around her urging her on. Her sweet soft moans are so fucking erotic, but I want to hear her scream.

"Cum on my cock, Baby." I demand and I feel her inner walls clamp down onto my dick. It is so fucking hot the way she responds to me.

"Oh god! Oh. Aghhh!" she screams before going limp in my arms. I relish in the warmth of her pussy juices that gush and coat my cock.

Goddamn it! That is hot as fuck.

Rolling her again onto her back, she tightens her legs around me. Tightly I grab hold of her ass and lift it up allowing me to pound that sweet pussy harder. The heavy ache in my balls becomes too much so I lean my head back and push hard one final time inside of her.

"Fuck! Aghhh!" I roar in release. I can't seem to stop pulsating inside of her. From the way I keep coming, I know that I must have filled the damn condom all the way up.

As I lay there still inside of her, everything changes for me. I have had earth shattering sex before, but absolutely nothing like this. Even when I lost my virginity, I'd never been slow and gentle with anyone. Before her, I hadn't cared if it was their first time or hundredth time. All I cared about was fucking them senseless and I sure as hell didn't take into consideration if they were comfortable while I did it. The more pain I inflict means more pleasure for me.

I know that I don't know anything about this girl, but I feel as if I have some type of connection with her. If you asked me to explain it, I'd have no way in fuck to do so. I want her in a way I've never wanted anyone before. I want to explore her body and push her to her limits. Now that I have claimed her, I will own her in every way.

Raven winces when I ease out of her. The bright red blood on the condom catches my attention once more, reminding me of what I had just taken from her. Pride fills my body knowing that I had been the first to lay stake to her sweet pussy. She has no idea the things I have in store for her the next fourteen days.

Tossing the condom aside, I gaze back down on her.

Goddamnit! I want her again.

The way she is laying is making me hard all over again. I can't do that again to her tonight. She isn't ready. I tenderly pull up the sheets to cover her body. It doesn't seem right to leave her exposed.

Shit! What is wrong with me? Why do I even care?

“Wait until I leave the room and you may remove the blindfold and leave. I will be in contact with you,” I say as I pull up my pants and exit the room. Once I’m on the other side of the door, I lean my head back against it and try to catch my breath. This is only day one and I don’t know if I will ever get enough of her.

Chapter Nine

Blaire

I nearly jump out of my skin when I hear the door shut in the room. No matter what I do, I can't seem to stop shaking. I know the reasons that I had done what I had, but he doesn't. He thinks I am just some whore now who had been willing to sell her virginity away for an ass load of cash. I can't worry about what he or anyone thinks of me; this had to be done.

Reaching my trembling hands around my head, I manage to untie the wet silk from my face. It takes me a few minutes before my eyes readjust to the dim light in the room, so I blink hard a few times to try to clear my vision. Feeling a bit sore, I ease myself off the bed and walk over to recover my robe and things from the floor. As I tie the sash around my waist, I can't help but blush at the things I had just done in this room.

Turning the knob to exit the room, I ignore the stares I get as I leave. I can hear the girls whispering and giggling nearby. I'm sure they wonder why I had finally become desperate enough to finally go into that room. I keep my head down and hurriedly make my way to the door beside the stage. Wasting no time, I hurry to the shower and turn on the water as hot as the temperature will go. With the thick rising steam surrounds me, I step beneath the stream of water.

Repeatedly, I scrub my skin as hard as I can, trying desperately to rid myself of the dirtiness I feel. My skin is raw from the force of the loofah. Throwing it down on the floor, I know it is useless. No matter what I do, I can't scrub the sluttiness off of me. Leaning my head against the cold tile, I glance down and see the light pink stream that trickles down my leg. I watch as it trickles off my foot and swirls around the drain. There it is. Vivid proof that I've lost something that I can never get back. My innocence is forever gone; hell, maybe it had been long before I ever walked in that room. Sliding down to the cold hard shower floor, I allow myself to cry and mourn the loss of something I had held so precious to me. I just pray it was all worth it.

After managing to dress and return to the hospital. I make my way to check on my mom once more before settling in for the night in the designated sleeping area for critical care patients' families. I only hope that tomorrow morning I feel less used than I do right now. I am honestly relieved that my mother can't see the whore I have become.

Day 2

The next day comes and goes faster than I could have ever imagined. All day long, I think that I will hear something from the Mr. R, but I don't.

Who is he anyway? And why does he call himself that? I don't have much room to speak about alter names; I live behind one too. Life for me is safer that way. Nobody knows the real me and I don't want them to.

I stop by our apartment to grab some more of my things and to take a quick shower. Dropping my keys and mail on the side table, I frown at the emptiness of the place. The least amount of time I spend here, the better, so I hurry to get what I need to do done. I pack extra clothes so I that I won't have to come back here for a few days.

Stopping by to check on my elderly neighbor, I give her a little bit of cash to put on her groceries this week. I don't have time to do the shopping for her today. I'm hoping she can manage on her own this time. She fights me on taking the money as she always does, and then awards me with a huge basket of fresh blueberry muffins. My stomach grumbles at the delicious aroma. They are my mom's favorite, so I accept them. I don't want to hurt her feelings or let her know just how bad my mom is this time. Stealing one from the basket, I tuck a few in my bag for later and decide to give the rest to the nurses back at the hospital. I only hope when I get there that Dr. Flannery doesn't approach me again about the money. I don't know what I will tell him if he does.

My mind suddenly races with terrifying thoughts.

What if he never pays me? What if I just let a stranger take my innocence for nothing? What will I do when it comes time for the surgery and there is nothing to pay them with? How can I be so stupid as to trust him at his word?

Jaxxon

I hadn't slept a damn wink all night.

I want her. I need her.

All I want to do this morning is lay in bed and fantasize about her. What the fuck is going on with me? I have grown so weak already. I can't allow this to continue.

Looking over at my phone, I see it's almost time to get up. Feeling exhausted, I roughly throw back the covers and sit up, cradling my throbbing head in my hands.

Damn Dr. Flannery and his early morning meetings!

Apparently, he has a patient who is a perfect candidate for trying the new valve we have just patented. I have to meet with him today to discuss the business end of things in order to get everything ready for the surgery to be performed.

The moment I arrive on the cardiac floor, I find him waiting on me. Quickly, he begins filling me in on the patient and her condition while motioning for me on into the room on the far corridor. When I see our patients first hand, I always get see the good things that my company does. But this time, as I look down at the pale woman lying on the bed, I feel more drawn to her case. I can't help but sense the coldness and insensitivity in the Doctor's voice when he spoke about her condition. It is as if he really is more concerned about this surgery being a success for him and not her. He places more value on his reputation as a renowned and distinguished heart surgeon than he does saving this woman's life.

What a fucking bastard!

I assure him we will have everything he will need in time for the surgery and he nods in approval. My company has made him a very wealthy man over the past few years and this particular surgery will prove to be no different. Shaking his hand, I make my way out of the room but am halted the moment I see her turning the corner. Raven.

Shit! She's here. What the fuck is she doing in this hospital? Pushing past the nurse in front of me, I duck into the nearest storage closet and hide. Luckily, the door has a small rectangular window, so I peek around to see if she is gone. Great! She isn't.

Dressed in a tight pale blue sweater and ass hugging jeans, Raven looks every bit as delicious as she did last night … well, almost. (Naked and blindfolded is definitely the better look for this girl.) Carrying a basket, I watch as she sits it on the nurses' station table and smiles at the lady behind the desk. The lady stands and comes around to hug Raven before motioning for the other nurses to join in on what looks to be muffins.

Is she a candy stripper or something? I can't wrap my mind around why she is here, especially this early in the morning.

Finally, Raven waves goodbye to the nurses and leaves.

Thank God!

Slowly, I open the door and look cautiously around the hallway. When I don't spot her, I deem it safe to exit. I have just made it to the nurses' station when I hear her voice. Quickly, I turn around and face the nurse at the station who returns my look with a flirtatious grin. I force a smile back at her and divert my eyes as she shoves out her chest at me. Ignoring her antics only makes seems to piss her off. With a loud huff, she shoves away from her desk and leaves. I lean into the counter of the desk and zone in on the conversation that is going on nearby.

"Blaire, I thought I made myself very clear yesterday."

Blaire. I love her real name.

"I am afraid that if you do not pay the upfront fee, I will be forced to remove your mother from the surgery schedule."

This is why she needed the money! Oh how I had misjudged this girl!

"Dr. Flannery, I assure you I will have the money to you. Just please don't remove my mom from the list." She says, her voice trembling.

What a fucking asshole! Did he really just threaten to remove her mother from his surgery schedule? My company is funding this surgery and he has no right to ask her for a fee. Had I known that this is why she needed the money, I wouldn't have been so ugly with her about it. I, like usual, have unfairly assumed the worst in her just as I do everyone else. It comes with being my father's son. It's why I seek the control I do.

"You have until noon tomorrow, Ms. Michaels. No exceptions." Dr. Flannery says before walking away. I watch her face drop and her dark eyes grow sad. The lost look on her face mixed with the heaviness of her shoulders sends a gut wrenching blow to my stomach.

I swear I am going to beat the fucking shit out of him for talking to her like this!

With a sad look on her beautiful face, she slowly turns and begins walking into the same room where I had been earlier with Dr. Flannery. Of course! Ms. Michaels had been the patient's name that will be the first recipient of the new synthetic valve that we are marketing. I can't believe of all people who could be receiving this valve that it is her mother. This is all just way too coincidental.

Dr. Flannery turns the corner at the nurses' station and meets my harsh stare head on.

"Mr. Ryder, I thought you had already left."

"You and I are about to have a little talk. I think that it may be one you'd prefer to have behind closed doors." I spit at him.

Looking at me as if I have suddenly grown three heads, he nods, motions for me to join him in the nearby vacant room, and closes the door behind us.

"What the hell were you just talking about?" I waste no time attacking him.

"I'm sorry, Mr. Ryder, but you have me at an advantage."

"The girl I just overheard you talking to. I thought her mother's surgery was definite."

"Yes, of course it is. You and I had discussed all of that this morning."

"That is what I though too. So why were you threatening to cancel it just now?" I ask him, now fuming.

"Calm down, Mr. Ryder. Ms. Michaels merely needed reminding about my fee."

"She does know this is an experimental surgery sponsored by Ryder Technology correct? You shouldn't have any fee involved in this!"

"Your company covers the fees for the surgery, but not for this patient's after care. I didn't get where I am in this business by working for charity cases."

"No. You got where you are in this business because my company funded you. Have you been asking for fees from all your patients?"

"Mr. Ryder… Jaxxon, I really don't see what the problem is. You are a cut throat businessman yourself."

"You should never make yourself rich off people who can't afford your care!" I turn in disgust and run my hand through my tousled hair, turning back around to face him.

"Jesus! Have you been doing this all along?" I ask and he doesn't even offer me an answer.

“From this point on, Ms. Michaels’ care will be completely taken care of by my company. You will not accept a dime from her daughter. If I hear of you threatening anyone again because of payment, I will make sure Ryder Technology finds another surgeon. Do we understand each other?”

“Yes, we understand each other perfectly,” he grits through angry teeth.

Angrily, I storm through the hallway. Taking the nearby stairwell, I don’t even bother waiting on the elevator. Once I reach the garage level, I am still seeping with anger. I don’t know who I am pissed at more, Dr. Flannery, her, or me. I hit my fob and slam my car door. FUCK!

This girl is driving me insane, and better yet, I am letting her. This has got to stop right now and I know just the way to remind her of who is in charge.

Phoning my accountant, I have her money wired to the bank account I had acquired through a little digging around. I make the amount for much more than we had originally discussed, but I have my reasons. Having her any way and any time I want for the next couple of weeks will be worth every single penny.

Chapter Ten

Blaire

Sleeping in a hospital is a joke. Glancing up at the clock on the waiting room wall, I see that is almost six in the morning. Some people around me still are sleeping on their designated lounger while others are beginning to stir. This is certainly not the most comfortable place to sleep, but there is no way I can stay in our little apartment without my mom being there.

Grabbing the bag beside my chair, I make my way to the community showers to dress for the day. After securing my long hair back into a ponytail, I decide to skip the makeup and head downstairs to grab some breakfast from the cafeteria in the basement level of the hospital. Since I had paid the hospital virtually every dime I had yesterday as a small installment, I need to stop by the ATM for a little bit of cash. As I select the twenty-dollar amount to withdraw, I silently pray the money is in there. While it begins dispensing my money, I hold my breath and prepare to cringe before looking down at the receipt in my hands. (I always hate seeing just how broke I am painted in black and white).

What the hell?

My eyes nearly bulge out of my head when I see the amount of my balance. I find myself shaking so badly that I have to grip the wall for support. $100,392.38. He had put over a hundred grand in my account! How did he even know who I am, much less my bank account information? I don't even realize I am walking in a daze until I've already passed the cafeteria. My stomach is doing summersaults too much for me to chance putting anything on it anyways.

Finding the first place I can, I collapse into the seat and try to catch my breath. I pull out the receipt and look down at it once more. Nope. I hadn't imagined it. This has to be some sort of bank error but it is too early for me to call them to check it out. Great! Just one more thing I have to do today.

My phone begins vibrating in my coat pocket and startles me. I am terrified to answer it because the only call I would get this early would be from the hospital. Gripping the phone tightly in my hand, I close my eyes and answer the call.

"Hello?"

"Hello, Raven," his sexy voice sends a voltage all the way down to my lower region. "You will be receiving a text of an address. I expect you to be at that location in less than twenty minutes. It is time we made our agreement official."

The line goes dead but then my phone alerts me to an incoming text message. Saving the message, I realize that the address is all the way across town from where I am. There is no way I can be there in twenty minutes if I drive through this traffic. Panicked, I grab my purse and head downstairs to hail a cab. Taking one is my only chance of being there on time.

Once I get to the designated address, I am confused. It is an abandoned parking lot. A familiar black, sleek Range Rover awaits with the same short driver standing beside the door. Studying the back passenger, side door, I wonder if this time Mr. R is in the back seat.

Handing the cab driver the entire twenty dollars I'd just withdrawn, I make my way over to where the driver is standing. He nods and gives me a kind smile. I can't see his eyes because they are hid behind thick aviator glasses. The driver opens the back door for me and motions me inside. Once again, I see that I am alone with a black silk blindfold on the seat.

"This time, I will be securing it, Miss." He explains and I nod, handing it to him. Once he secures it, he closes the door and moments later, he is driving us. I remember watching a movie once where the kidnapped victim had memorized every turn and detail of the road when they were in the trunk of a car. But after the first two turns, I am completely lost as to where we are or where we are going. Never believe what you see in the movies.

After what seems like a long time, the vehicle stops, and the driver helps me out of the SUV. Gently he takes my arm, leading me into some sort of building. We take an elevator up quite a ways and then we continue down a long hallway of some sort. I hear the door in front of me open and close. He pulls the blindfold down and I squint at the bright light of the room.

I can't believe this view! Who could ever work in a place like this? I'd never get anything accomplished from staring out the window all day! I bet this has a phenomenal view of the city at night. I am instantly snapped away from my thoughts when I hear my name echo across the huge open space.

"Hello Raven." Mr. R says and I notice him sitting in a chair facing the windows on the far end of room.

My core throbs. How does he do that to me? I can't be normal.

"Hello." I reply, still hoping he is about to turn around in the chair. He doesn't.

"Have a seat, please." He orders and I walk towards the long table in the room. Instantly, I see a small box and a thick stack of papers that appear to be an agreement of some sort. The contract.

"You will see two contracts in front of you. One is your copy; the other one belongs to me. I have already signed both copies. Our agreement will be official once you've signed them. I trust you have received your payment."

"Yes, but there must be some mistake. It is more than we had agreed upon."

"I have my reasons, Raven. I didn't feel like what you asked was a fair price. Not for what I have in store for you," he says with coldness in his voice.

Please turn around so I can see you!

Overwhelmed, I stare down at the papers in front of me. Flipping through the pages, I become slightly overwhelmed at all of the amendments as I read through a few of them.

"Yes, I am a ruthless business man, Raven. I get what I want when I want it. You'll find that I am not tolerant nor am I patient. I don't apologize for that. As my submissive, I'll expect you to live up to that contract in every way."

"There is so much in here. I can't possibly read through every detail that quickly, Mr. R."

"You will look over it now! If you have any questions or concerns, then voice them to me before you leave. Once you sign, there is no going back. You will either accept or reject the contract. There will be no negotiations in this deal. As I said before, I am not a patient man, Raven. I also believe I told you before that I expected you to call me Sir!"

"Yes, Sir," I reply, trying to swallow down the fear in my throat. Turning the page bold print catches my attention.

SPECIFICATIONS:

I. All physical and sexual encounters between submissive and Dominant will only occur when submissive is blindfolded. Identity of Dominant is to remain anonymous. Any failure to comply with this will result in immediate termination of contract.

II. Submissive will only wear skirts or dresses for the entire length of contract. No pants or jeans are allowed.

III. Submissive will be available 24 hours a day, 7 days a week. A phone will be provided for submissive by Dominant and is to be kept on at all times. Any failure to comply with any of these specifications will result in IMMEDIATE termination of contract.

"The part about the phone. What if something happens and I can't take the call?" I ask him, referring to the times I'm at the hospital visiting or at work.

"It will be a violation of our contract."

"But, Sir, I-," I start to explain, but he cuts me off.

"If I call, you answer. NO exceptions!" I jump at his words and shove the fear aside in order to return to reading.

As I continue looking through each amendment, I feel my face begin blushing. Does he honestly expect me to do all of these things? Better yet, can I do all of this? When I read further down, I see several references to sexual positions and devices. The thought of a few of these has me intrigued and even sends my head in a fantasy scenario.

My fantasy ends when I see the word ***PUNISHMENT*** in bold print. Scanning the listed types of punishments, I shudder at the words before me.

Belt, Crop, Caning, Muzzle, Whip…

There is no fucking way I will allow him to do any of that to me!

"Will you really beat me if I refuse something?"

"That all depends. Are you already thinking you will deny me of something I ask?"

"No, Sir. I'm just not sure about some of these things."

"Don't defy me and you will have nothing to worry about."

That is yet to be seen. Part of my body already wants to defy him. My mind thinks about the spanking he gave me the other night and I feel my clit throb at the memory. Crossing my long legs, I squirm a bit in my seat. There is something definitely wrong with me to find anything about being punished as being erotic. I can take most of these punishments, but I don't think I can handle the cane.

My eyes read further down to ***LIMITS*** and I spot the words ***SAFEWORD***. I've heard of this in the books I've read and from some of the girls who work at the club. I wouldn't even know what to come up with for a word.

Skipping over more details, I jump to the last page and sign my name, repeating the same to the other contract. If I don't sign, the deal is off. I can't risk that, so I sign.

"Alright, I'm done," I say, sitting down my pen.

"Already? Are you sure about that?" He asks with humor in his voice.

"Yes, Sir."

"I'm not so sure that you are," he replies, now with more yearning in his voice. I don't respond to his comment.

"Tell me, Raven, are you on the pill?"

"Yes, Sir. I've been on it for a while now." I don't bother explaining to him the reasons I am on it. Working at the club, I'd been too panicked I would be attacked by one of the men. It's a safety thing for me.

"Excellent. In that contract, you will find my latest medical testing. I have a clean bill of health. I assume you understand you are to be mine exclusively. I will not have you sharing another man's bed."

"That won't be a problem. I have only ever been with you, Sir."

"Excellent. So what are you wearing right now?"

"Um, I'm wearing a yellow sundress." I stutter nervously.

Why does that matter?

"Very good. That will make this next part much easier."

"What part?"

"Pick up the pen, Raven." Confused, I hesitate to move.

"NOW!"

I reach out in front of me and take the long thick fountain pen back in my hand.

"Lean back in the chair and ease the pen inside of you."

What the fuck did he just ask me to do?

Holding up the silver pen in front of me, I nervously examine it. Engraved letters, Congratulations J.R. are etched into the side. Mentally, I try to figure out what the letters stand for, but his voice sends me jumping.

"I *said* put the pen inside of you!"

Feeling embarrassed, I lean back and spread my legs.

Dear God, I can't believe that I'm doing this right now.

Pushing my pink thong aside, my wet folds embrace the cool metal as I guide it on in me.

"I want you to fuck yourself with it and make you come," he demands.

I can't do this! This is ridiculous.

"I said now! I want to hear you scream as you come hard on that pen!"

Increasing my movements, I feel the tip where the clip is attached tease my sweet spot. Who would have ever thought this would feel so damn good. I can feel it building so I push it deeper inside.

"That's right, Baby. Fuck yourself hard! I want your cum coating my pen!"

His words spiral me out of control.

"Oh. My. God!" My warm release drips down my fingertips as I ride out my orgasm. I can hear his ragged breathing from all the way across the room.

"Very good, Raven. Now, place it back on the table," he manages to say breathlessly.

Straightening up in the chair, I smooth back my hair and pull down my skirt. Still reeling from my intense orgasm, I place the pen back in front of me.

It glistens in the light from my juices. Heat overtakes my face as I grow more embarrassed.

"I suggest you take the contract home and study it carefully so that you can prepare for what to expect. Remember, you have signed it. For the remainder of these next two weeks, you are mine. It's officially right there in black and white now. The box beside of you is your new phone. Keep it with you and on at all times!"

"Parker, please escort my guest back to her home."

"No Sir, that won't be necessary. I work tonight."

"Very well, then. Parker will take you wherever you need to go."

Parker emerges carrying the blindfold in his hands. Tying it tightly around my face, he lifts my arm and pulls me to my feet. Suddenly, I hear footsteps walking toward us. Parker stops and releases my hand. I feel a thumb as it glides across my lower lip. A volt of energy surges through me and radiates deep down to my lower region.

"I look forward to when we meet again," he whispers against my lips. His delicious flavor of cinnamon fills my nose. I want him to kiss me, but he doesn't. Tenderly, he tucks my hair behind my ear and then I feel Parker take my arm again. My legs are so weak from his encounter that I'm relieved to be relying on him to help me out of here. I have no explanation for the way he makes me feel nor for the things that I want him to do to me. I don't know what happened in there, but I am fairly certain that I just signed my soul away to the devil.

Jaxxon

I miss her the minute she walks out the door. There is no denying that she and I share an undeniable connection. One that I'm sure will be my undoing. Now that I have her name on this contract, I smile. She is officially mine. Eyeing my silver pen on the wooden table, I feel my dick grow hard. Moving to the desk, I quickly pick it up and feel her slick wetness that still saturates it. I smell her delicious scent as I move it beneath my nose. Hungrily, I open my mouth and slowly guide it between my lips, savoring her sweet flavor as it saturates my tongue. As I pull it back out, I look back down at it in my hand, staring at the etching Congratulations J.R.

Moving back over to my desk, I sit down, still studying it in my hand.

I hate this pen.

It represents every insincere thing about my father. This had been my graduation present from college. A stupid forty-dollar pen. Not to mention, it had been picked out and delivered by one of his many suckataries. I'm sure it's easy to get why I call them that. Over the years, they've spent a lot of time on their knees to keep their jobs.

Lifting up the picture frame on my desk, I smile warmly down at it. I will forever remember my graduation day. My grandfather had bought me my first Porsche as a surprise. My asshole father had huffed saying how impractical it is to own one. The car didn't mean anything to me. My grandfather being there did. Thankfully, I have this picture on my desk immortalizing the moment.

The one simple word etched on this pen is the one word he has never said to me. Congratulations. I laugh to myself. As funny as it is, I'm sure he didn't even plan on it being written on this gift. Hell, he'd never even known that he'd given it to me in the first place. Running the metal underneath my nose once more, I can still smell her. My dick instantly points to the Heavens above, pressing hard against the seam of my zipper. Yes, this just became my favorite pen. She has taken a horrible memory and replaced it with one that I will never forget.

Walking over to the bar in my office, I pour a large glass of bourbon before moving to the long wall of windows.

I love living here in this building.

The entire top three floors of this ten-story building are occupied solely by me. All other floors below that are luxury apartments, and are managed by one of my best friends, Marcus. Even though I own the building, I give him 100 percent of the profits just to run the place. It does quite well for him and it saves me the headache of dealing with tenants. My privacy is the only thing I have ever asked in return and Marcus has always made sure to respect that.

The eighth floor is a smaller version of my penthouse. I keep it available for when my friends stay from out of town maybe a few weeks out of the year. The ninth floor, or Level Nine as I call it, is the floor that I play on. It is where I have my submissives delivered to when I feel the need to feed the demon inside. The floor is divided into several different rooms, as well as a large control room. Each place houses different devices for pleasure and pain. I should call this floor Hell. It is, after all, where my demon unleashes itself upon its prey. Nothing will satisfy it more than when I bring her here to feed it.

The sooner the better.

The evening sky beams its warm pink hues in the sky bidding the sun farewell. I think I shall pay Ms. Raven a visit tonight at the club. My body craves to be near her. Images of her on stage only make me hungrier for her.

Tonight, I'll be near my Raven again.

Chapter Eleven

Blaire

I don't want to work tonight, but I can't risk losing this job. In this business, if you miss too much work you are easily replaced by another set of tits or ass. Luckily, I bypass having to speak with Honey tonight in the dressing room. No one here knows anything about my personal life or me. They do know that I've never missed a day of work in the six months I'd been here.

"Raven! We have a pretty large bachelor party here tonight so Mike wants you up early on the second set." One of the bouncers yells into the room.

"Got it!" I yell back as I frantically finish getting ready. I don't know what to wear tonight, but I'm drawn to do something to match my dark mood. Searching my wardrobe, I hold up just the right one. All the men really seem to really love this little black leather number. Hooking the leather corset into place, I slide into the lace panties and hook the black fishnets into position. Stepping into my black leather thigh high boots, I quickly zip them up and move back to the dressing table.

Playing up my eyes with dark eye shadow, I finish off my look with my fire engine red lipstick. Adding a thick layer of high gloss to my lips, I toss the tube back into my makeup kit and run my hands through my long waves, fluffing out my hair a bit more.

"God! They are animals out there tonight!" Honey's voice unexpectedly appears behind me.

"Hey, babe! I've missed you," she says as she plops into her seat beside me. I hadn't really thought about what to say to her. My issues with her are my own problem, not really hers.

"Family emergency. I'm back now."

"Is everything alright?" she looks at me with concern in her eyes. I've never told her anything much about me and I don't like starting to now.

"Um, yeah. It's gonna be fine," I reply.

"RAVEN! You're up!"

"Go get 'em girl!" Honey says as she playfully slaps my behind.

"Alright guys, you will all need to be heading to church repenting after this one! Let's give it up for our girl RAVEN!"

Marilyn Manson's "Personal Jesus" blares through the speakers as the stage lights dance around me. I am blinded against the crowd. The switch from Blaire to Raven takes over just as I turn to take hold of the pole. Tonight, they get the anger that fills my soul. Swinging my body around the metal, I thrust my hips around, grinding on the pole before shimmying down to the floor. Wrapping my legs tightly around the steel, I make my journey upwards, climbing higher and higher into the air. Freefalling backwards, I firmly squeeze my thighs and slide down the pole, remaining upside down.

Flipping back over, I spread my legs wide for the crowd. Men are screaming for more while that lovely green paper flies all around below me. Setting myself back on the floor, I drop down to make my way on all fours, crawling down the length of stage. I dare a closer than normal proximity to the men on the side. Usually, I never let them touch me, but Mike wants us to be kinder and friendlier to the bachelor parties that come in here. Tonight, I bravely decide to give them a closer view. The men touch my thighs and tuck money in my garters and underwear.

Inching backwards to a safer distance, I reach in front of me and unclasp the hook on the front the corset. Something is different this time and it causes me to hesitate. The men don't like being teased and they scream louder at me to take it off for them.

"Come on, Baby, show us those tits! Bring your fine ass over here so I can taste that pussy," the vulgarities fly around me.

Why is this so hard this time? Why can't I do this?

Pushing back the emotions raging inside of me, I drop my top and allow my breasts to fall free. I shove them up with my hands as I fall to my knees. Raising my hands to lift my dark curls, I slowly release my hair allowing it to cascade down my back. Arching my body against the floor, I rock my hips to the loud beats around me. For a moment, I am lost in the song's lyrics. When I finally open my troubled eyes, they immediately lock with the Beautiful Man from the other night.

Holy-damn-fuck-shit!

His eyes are hungry and extraordinarily angry. I can't break his stare so I once again do the unthinkable. I slide my hand down my body and in between my legs. His brows furrow as he squirms in his seat.

Good. It's working.

But then, just as I am proud of myself for making him desire me, he jumps up and storms off, leaving me nervous, confused, and embarrassed to finish my number on stage.

The music ends and I lift my body up to see that I am surrounded in mounds of cash. Whistles and catcalls fill the air as I shove the money in my bag before exiting the stage. I think this is the most money I've ever made on one set since I've been here.

Before walking through the backstage door, I brave another glance around the room. Beautiful Man is gone. Maybe tonight he'd been just a figment of my imagination; maybe he'd save me from my insanity.

Jaxxon

Damn it! I thought I could handle her doing this, but I can't. She has no idea the need and desire I'd felt when she locked eyes with mine. I wanted her so fucking much that I about came in my damn pants. Something happened when I saw her up on that stage and I damned sure hadn't expected it to. Tonight, instead of just watching her dance, I had zoned in on how the men around the room lusted for her. I heard every single nasty comment they shouted at her. Yeah, I'd fucking hated every goddamned second of it. She belongs to me, not to them. Her body is for my eyes, not theirs. I had to get out of here before I killed every one of these horny sons of bitches.

The night air hits my face, but I can still hear the men scream for her all the way outside. Punching the brick on the building, I feel the warm blood from where I've broken my skin. This will never happen again. After tonight, she will never set another foot on that stage. Pushing my way back inside, I find the owner and make him a deal that he can't refuse.

A few drinks and a handshake later, I've become the new official owner of Club Climax. And my manager, Mike, is about to fire one of most valuable employees.

Blaire

I have just finished getting ready for my second set when Mike comes into the dressing room. On nights like these, it is highly unusual for him to leave the front of the club. Automatically, his presence confuses me. "Lacey, you're up next. Raven, I need to speak to you."

"But Mike, I'm up next," I explain, but he waves me to join him.

"Looks like Little Miss Perfect just got in trouble," Lacey says and the other girls begin laughing. Everyone except Honey, that is.

"Fuck off, Lacey!" Honey defends me, forcing me a pained smile. So much of her I will never understand. Even after what had happened with her and Beautiful Man, I still know she has my back.

My legs begin wobbling as I nervously walk to the other room where he is waiting. I don't understand what this could possibly be about.

"Look, Raven. I hate to do this to you, especially now and all, but I'm having to let you go."

"What? Mike! I am sorry I missed the other day. I will make it up, I swear. You know I need this job right now more than ever. Please!" I beg him, but he holds his hands up to stop me from saying anything more.

"You're a sweet girl, Raven. You don't need to be in a place like this anyways. Do something better than this with your life."

"I don't understand. Why are you doing this?" I'm crying hysterically now. There is no way I can't make it without this job.

"I'm sorry, Raven." He says, leaving me standing in the side storage closet crying all alone.

When I finally emerge from the room, everyone turns and stares. Some are laughing while others just whisper. I'm in such a shocked state that I don't know what to do. Dazed, I take my bag and pull out my jeans and sweatshirt. Quickly changing, I then walk over to my designated wardrobe area.

Yanking the clothes off the hangers, I violently shove them into my bag, tossing along shoes and other accessories. I want to just rip all of it into shreds at this point. I don't have room in my bag for my angel wings so I throw them into Honey's pile next to my section. Leaving, I grab for my makeup kit on the counter and wipe the tears away from the back of my hand. As I walk away, I glance up and catch a glimpse of myself in the long mirror on the wall. The split glass is quite fitting since that is how I feel. Broken. My thick heavy eye shadow is now smeared everywhere down my face. I look horrific and I don't give a fuck. All I want to do is to leave and pretend that I had never walked into this club in the first place. It has already robbed me of so much.

Cursing the air before me, I stagger across the pavement of the club parking lot still in these tall ass stilettos. "Fuck!" I scream as my ankle twists, causing me to stumble. Mike is too damn cheap to fill in these holes! The pavement crunches behind me. I spin around, raising up my heavy bag ready to punch the asshole who is creeping up on me.

I see him emerge from the shadows and feel my chest tighten. It is as if every single ounce of air just got sucked out of my body. His eyes are so powerful that they paralyze me in my spot. My limp arm drops the heavy weight beside me, nearly taking my limp body down with it. We stare at each other for what seems like forever. And just like that, he turns and walks away, leaving me there in a shaking nervous mess.

The moment my feet begin working again, I run to my car and throw my bag into the back seat. When I glance in the rearview mirror, I expect to see him there but he isn't. As fast as possible, I barrel out this place, trying to leave the pain and regret there along with it.

Chapter Thirteen

Day 4

Blaire

Cry. That's all I ever seem to do anymore as if crying does me any good. People around me don't pay me any mind. I guess they think it's natural to be upset at this place. It's certainly not the happiest place for any of us to be right now.

All night long, I had held onto my pillow as the tears soaked the cotton pillowcase. I have no job, my bills are going to pile up, and, worst of all, my mom is having her surgery tomorrow. I know it is her only hope, but I also know it is also a risky and dangerous procedure, one with a long list of bad outcome scenarios. The thought of her not making it tears my soul out. That is, if I even have one left in me now.

Splashing cold water on my face, I shuffle around the clothes in my bag searching for something to wear. My hands slide across something and I quickly realize it's the contract he gave me yesterday. I'd read over it a bit last night before I fell asleep and cursed myself for not reading it more carefully before I had signed it. Suddenly, I remember what it had said about my attire.

A dress or a skirt. Shit!

I dig deeper in the bag. Thankfully, I have packed an extra skirt in here with my other things to wear today. Taking a little extra time, I dress and add makeup to cover up my puffy eyes. Checking my bag into my assigned storage locker, I toss the lock in my purse and head upstairs to check on my mom.

You'd think this would get easier, but it doesn't. Every time I walk in her room, I am overwhelmed at the sight of her. The machines that keep her breathing and the fluids that pump inside her keep her body fed. Each visit I have with her, she looks weaker and paler than the time before. I just want my mom back. I miss her voice; I miss her laugh. Squeezing her cold hand, I lean in and place a kiss on her forehead.

"I'm here, Mom. Stay with me!"

Continuing with my normal routine, I alternate rubbing her feet and her hands with her favorite lotion. The room smells of raspberry vanilla when I'm done. I sit beside the bed and begin reading to her. With her eyes so weak, she'd always loved it when I'd do this at home. I am just finishing her favorite chapter of The Notebook when a knock on the door interrupts me. Susan, one of my mom's favorite nurses on this floor, peeps her head in and smiles at me.

"Hi, Blaire. We're needing to get your mom ready to run a group of final tests for surgery tomorrow. It may be a while so why don't you go home and get some rest. You look exhausted."

A nap? Sleep? What exactly is that? It's been so long since I've slept solid I'd forgotten. Exhaustion is just something I deal with.

"Thanks Susan. I've got some errands I need to do anyways." I reply. I have still have to take care of arranging for the bank to transfer the money to pay off my mom's hospital bill. I kiss my mom goodbye and Susan gives me a sympathetic smile.

"We'll take good care of her," she promises.

I nod and pick up my purse to leave. As I wait for the elevator to arrive, I study the speckled tiles of the hospital floor. I manage to count forty-six specks before the familiar ping sounds its arrival. I watch my reflection distort as the steel doors open. Instantly, the air electrifies me sending goose bumps all the way down my spine.

I dare a glance upwards and lock eyes with the last person on Earth I'd ever expect to see here. Beautiful man. Sharply dressed in an expensive charcoal gray designer suit with a dark crimson silk tie, he exudes power and wealth. His dark eyes pierce me, silently commanding me forward. Every single inch of my body is on fire and I haven't even touched him. It terrifies me to think what would ever happen if I ever do.

I can't speak.

I can't breathe.

I can't move.

Smiling he holds the elevator door, preventing it from closing.

Sweet Jesus! Why does he have to have a smile like that! It's simply not fair.

I want to walk forward, but I can't. Shyly smiling back at him, my eyes drop to the floor and I step forward into the elevator with him. The doors shut behind me and I panic.

Shit!

Can I be in this closed space with him, without my body combusting into flames?

"Thank you, Sir." I say, catching myself in the way I'd just addressed him. Mr. R's rules have overtaken me, I suppose. His gorgeous dark eyes burn with intensity; the sly smile he rewards me with is lethal. Looking down, I swallow the huge lump in my throat and nervously play with the bracelet on my wrist. When I look back up, he is still staring at me.

Damn my body! Damn him! Why is he even here at this place anyways?

I try to keep staring ahead, but my eyes are fighting some unforeseen force. I do what every smart girl does, the one thing that men never can seem to do without turning their head, I use my supersonic peripheral vision. Everything about him is complete and utter perfection. Greek Gods would bow at this man's feet. Hell, I can't even look at the man without blushing. I don't know why he is still studying me.

My mind wonders. Is he like Mr. R? Sure he is! Men like him need that power. I'm sure he has a long list of women he ties up and fucks. I grow sick at my stomach. Oh God. Jealousy overtakes me and I finally admit something to myself.

I want to be one of his women.

Sweat forms on my brow; my chest is burning from keeping in the breath I hadn't known I was holding.

Damn it! Why is it so fucking hot in this elevator?

Sex.

All I can think about is sex. For days now, I've fantasized about this man touching and fucking me. He has no idea the things I've done with another man, all while imagining he was the one doing it to my body instead. Every time Mr. R touches me, it is him. When Mr. R rams his cock inside of me, in my mind, it's him instead.

My face blushes at my memories. I shift my legs to ease the fullness in my lower region, my need for a release growing more and more unbearable by the second. This man is going to cause me to orgasm just by standing next to him. He is still waiting for me to look in his direction, but I can't. If I dare look back into his eyes, I will be lost. I want him to take me right now in this elevator. I don't care that he has had Honey. I want him, but he is too dangerous. Just like Mr. R, I will only ever be an easy meaningless fuck to Beautiful Man.

Knowing I have to distract myself for the few remaining floors, I pretend to search for my car keys in my purse, even though they've been in the inside pocket all along. Reaching in to retrieve them, the elevator slows, settling on the ground floor. He extends his hand out to allow me to exit first and I nervously step forward. I'm so clumsy that I trip on my first step, but his hands are there to catch me. The power in his touch overwhelms me, sending my keys flying out my hand, landing just beside my foot.

Once he steadies me, he bends down to pick up my keys, taking a moment to place his hand around my ankle. His gentle stroke of his finger across my foot is spellbinding. That one touch literally electrocutes my vagina. My body is shaking; I feel the warmth of his body as he stands to lean in closer. My clit throbs harder.

Oh, fuck!

Beautiful Man takes my hand into his. As if he wills me to do so, I open it. He slides my keys delicately across my palm and then shuts my fingers around them. Something about his touch is so familiar. Why? He looks deep into my eyes, virtually stripping my soul into and stealing my breath. Forcing my eyes away, I have to blink out of his hypnotic power. What just happened?

Sweet Jesus, I want him!

I've got to get the hell out of here before I throw myself on him and have my way. With wobbly knees and soaked panties, I bolt off the elevator and practically run out the front door of the hospital.

The warm beautiful sunlight feels heavenly on my face. I wish I could smile at it; I wish I had anything worth smiling about. No matter how hard I try, a black cloud always follows me, raining on any happiness I've ever managed to have in my life.

It's a long way to my car since I had to park so far away last night. I don't mind the walk. Right now, I need to clear my head and find peace. I think I know just the place. Shamefully, it has been a while since I have been there, but I think it is the only thing that can help me right now. My car finally starts after several attempts, and I circle the parking lot, heading somewhere I pray will help.

Jaxxon

I'm sure she thinks our meeting is by accident, but it certainly isn't. She needs to be tested. I need to know how she will respond to me. I need her to see how my body reacts to her. She needs to see what is right in front of her eyes now that the blindfold is off.

My plan is more than effective! She wants me just as much as

I want her. When she first stepped in this elevator, I didn't think I would be able to control myself from having what I want. What does that say about me? Who is testing whom here? I should have no problem staying in control, but it's becoming painfully obvious that my brilliant plan is backfiring right in my face.

As if I have some sort of mind power over her, I will her to look at me. I want her to feel me, to touch me. To know that I'm the one who makes her scream in pleasure. I want her to know that she is mine. I know it sounds stupid to admit, but I am becoming jealous of myself. When she knows me as Mr. R, she acts as if she wants him, but now, she acts as if she wants Jaxxon, too. Isn't it obvious? Can she not see that we are the same person?

When her keys drop, it gives me the perfect opportunity to test her a little more. I can smell her sweet desire blanketing the entire elevator. It makes my mouth drool, my cock twitch. She needs to be fucked. I need to fuck her. Perhaps then, she will recognize that I own her.

Do not touch her. You will not be able to suppress the desire.

Dropping to my knees, I fight it, but it's no use. I crave the feel of her skin. The moment I bend down, I catch a glimpse of the red mark on her ankle. Immediately, I know it is from the other night. I suppress the growl inside of me. My chest swells with pride that I've marked her. But sometimes pride blinds us, just like now. Before I even realize it, I have my hand on her ankle. Her skin sears me with desire, but I can't let go. I dare an upward glance of her fucking, long, gorgeous legs. Her beautiful body begins shaking and I smile. I've successfully placed her under my spell. Normally I would gloat because I've never met a woman who is immune to my charm. Until her, I've never been turned down. The only thing is that I've also never met a woman who has ever left me powerless. Blaire Michaels has officially brought me to my knees.

She is so lost in thought that she doesn't even notice that I'm following her. Settling into my car, I continue observing her from a safe distance. Adjusting my sunglasses, I put my car in gear and follow her out of the parking lot. We drive for a couple of miles before she pulls in front of a large, old church building and parks.

A church? Are you kidding me?

I certainly didn't see this one coming. Smiling devilishly, I devise another plan. I've tested her reaction to me. Now, it's time to test her loyalty.

Chapter Fourteen

Blaire

Perhaps it is the chaos that I call my life, or the desperation I have to plea for my soul, but for whatever reason, I find myself sitting in the back of this old church. Growing up, I always loved coming here with my mom on Sundays. The one hundred and twenty-year-old building is one of the oldest churches in our town and has been featured in many magazines for its amazing architectural designs. With its beautiful cathedral ceilings, carved wooden balcony, and gorgeous stained glass windows, I can’t picture a more perfect place for anyone to find solace. Closing my eyes, I take a deep breath, enjoying the silence around me. This is definitely what I need right now.

Since it is early in the afternoon, the church is virtually empty except for the two people in the front row. Not wanting to be seen, I opt to sit in the far corner near the wall. I haven’t been in this place for over a year, but everything still looks the same. Since I’ve started stripping, I’ve felt as if I don’t deserve passage through these doors. I feel like hypocrite being here. Even though my reasons for living this double life come with good intentions, I don’t really think that God sees it that way.

I straighten my skirt and bow my head. Before I can even begin my prayer, a quiet chirping in my coat pocket makes me scramble to keep from causing a scene. I know I should have silenced the phone while I am in church, but I can’t risk not answering him when he calls for me.

Turning my body to the side, I whisper, “Hello?”

"It is time to play, my pet."

"I can't. I'm at chur-"

I try to explain but he quickly snaps at me.

"Silence!" he roars at me. "I don't care *where* you are! You will do as I say! Is that understood?"

"Y-Yes, Sir," I reply as quietly as I can into the phone.

"Good. Very good, Raven. I would hate for us to have a problem with you understanding that. Did you wear a skirt like I asked?"

"Yes, Sir."

"Good girl. Are you sitting?"

"Yes, Sir."

"Such good manners, my beautiful girl. I want you to spread your legs open and run your hand up your thigh."

I hesitate and he growls into the phone, "Are you doing it?"

"Sir, I-,"

I begin speaking, but am cut off once again by him before I can argue.

"Do it!" he screams into the phone, sending fear through my body.

Looking around, I see that no one is paying me any attention. I don't bother looking up because I know the balcony is closed for future renovations, and no one is allowed up there. As I slide my hand underneath my skirt, a rush of guilt passes over me. For goodness sake, this is a church. This is so wrong! Just minutes ago, I walked in this place to find peace, and now I am touching myself. Reaching further up, I discover how wet his commanding voice has made me.

Yeah, I'm pretty sure I am going to Hell.

"You're already dripping wet for me, aren't you, Raven? Tell me the truth!"

“Yes,” I breathlessly answer him while continuing to swirl my fingers around my moist opening.

This is so unbelievably wrong, but feels so right.

God help me*! Does it ever feel so right!*

“Close your eyes. I want you to pretend that it’s me touching you. Imagine every movement of your fingers as being mine,” he orders, and I gasp into the phone.

Dear Lord! This is so unbelievably hot!

“That’s right, Baby. Feel that warm wet pussy. Do you want me to fuck you?”

“Yes, Sir.”

His breath quickly catches over the phone. I can hear just how turned on this is making him.

“I want you to stick two fingers inside of you and fuck yourself until you come. I want you to make your thighs drip! Do it now!”

And just like that, my body automatically obeys his every command. I find myself leaning back into the wooden church pew with my legs spread wide open, thrusting my fingers inside of my drenched hot opening. Over and over, I urge my fingers deeper inside until I feel my walls grip down hard. Growing even wetter, I bite down on my lip to hold in the scream that threatens to escape my lips.

Yes, I am definitely hell bound for this one!

His breathing quickens in the phone and drives me even more over the edge.

“Taste yourself, Raven. See how sweet that pussy of yours tastes.”

I am still in a daze from my orgasm, but I manage to pull my soaked fingers up to my mouth and ease them between my lips.

“Mmmmm,” I moan unknowingly into the phone.

“Raven?” he whispers, his breathing now erratic and

desperate. I know this is having just as much an effect on him as it is on me.

“Yes, Sir?” I reply and hear him let out a hiss and growl.

“Go to the ladies bathroom down the hall and face the wall. Do it NOW!” he demands and then the line goes dead.

What the hell? He’s here?

My body reacts before I have time to consider my actions. Without thinking, I jerk my head up just in time to catch the dark shadow move away from the light of the balcony overhead. He’s been watching me all along. Did he see me looking for him just then? I know I don’t have much time to follow his instructions.

Grabbing my coat and purse, I make my way to the bathroom in the front hallway of the church. The moment I am inside, I see that I am alone. Laying my things on the chair, I walk towards the long wall. Tracing my fingertips across the familiar flowers on the wallpaper, I smile. It’s been over twenty years, and they still haven’t changed this!

Suddenly, the door behind me opens and I feel the electrified shift in the air. It smolders with sex and desire so intense that it instantly causes my clit to begin throbbing. I don’t understand what is changing in me. It terrifies me how much my body needs him. Mr. R. inches closer and closer, his hypnotic spicy cologne filling my nose. No matter how badly I want to, I don’t dare turn around to face him. I know that it isn’t allowed. The loud click of the lock indicates that he means business. I hear the leather of his belt as he slides it through his pant loops.

“Keep facing forward, Raven! Put your hands on the wall! You know the rules! You forgot to bring your blindfold, didn’t you?”

“Yes, Sir. I’m sorry,” I reply as I place my hand on the crumbling, floral wallpapered wall. His hand inches underneath my skirt and he discovers that I’ve already removed my panties.

“Very good, Raven. What a little slut you are. You really should be ashamed that you made yourself come on that pew.”

My body sings its lustful melody. I want him inside of me.

"Spread those feet apart. I'm going to fuck you hard and quick! Don't hold ANYTHING back from me! I want to hear you scream to the Heavens above! I want God to see just what a dirty girl you really are! Trust me. He already knows that I'm going to make you come harder than you ever have in your life!"

I hear him jerk his zipper down and drop his pants. In one swift move, he grabs my hips, spreads my cheeks, and rams his long hard cock inside of me. This is the first time that I've felt him bare and I had no idea how magnificent it would feel. I can feel every ridge of his smoldering hot dick as it slides in and out of my wetness.

This feels so damn good!

With his free hand, he slips the brown leather belt around the base of my throat, pulling it hard against my skin. My head slings back and rests against the front of his forehead as he fucks me harder and harder from behind. My airway becomes restricted, making my world dizzy. I don't care. I just want more of him. The sweet, musky scent of sex flavors the air around us while the glorious sound of our skin slapping against one another echoes in the small bathroom.

Digging my fingernails into the crumbling floral wallpaper, delicious sensations ripple through my body. Waves of ecstasy wash over me. He releases the leather belt from around my neck and the metal buckle hits the floor beside me. I want to turn and see his face so badly, but I know better than to ever risk it. Reaching up, he wraps his hand around my long dark waves, forcefully yanking me back to him. He slowly breathes in my hair and a loud growl fills my ear. His free hand slides off the wall and lands on my ass. Two hard strikes to my skin, then his fucking becomes even more feral.

"Give me more of that ass!" he grits out as he yanks back violently on my hair.

The instant I push out my ass, I take all of him in the next forceful thrust. The wonderful sensation of holding all of him inside of me is mind blowing. My eyes roll in the back of my head when the tip of his cock presses hard into my cervix.

“Fuck, Baby! That’s it! Feel all of me!” He gasps and wraps his other hand around my waist.

“Oh God!” I yell as the orgasm erupts through my body. There is no way I can hold anything back. He owns my body.

“Go ahead and scream His name. Just remember, He isn’t the one making you come! I am!”

“Oh … my Aaghhh!” I scream louder, not caring who can hear me.

“Fuck!!” he shouts, coating my core with his hot seed.

I’ve never felt anything as erotic as his spurts of cum.

I can’t breathe. Every inch of my body is still on fire for him. He is gasping for air just as much as I am right now. I frown when he pulls out of me. Inside of me is the only place I want him to be. I know it is insane to say, but it’s as if he belongs there. Bracing myself against the wall, I catch myself before my knees give way. I expect to hear him begin dressing, but he doesn’t. Lifting up my curls, I feel him brush my hair to the side, exposing the skin of my bare back. I feel his lips lightly brush across my neck. My sex throbs, begging him to push back inside of me. His hot tongue traces across my neck and down to my shoulder.

“Raven, what are you doing to me?” he whispers so low that I wonder if I am even meant to hear it.

He blows across my skin where he’s licked, sending shivers all the way down my spine.

I want him. God help me, I do. How can I need him so much? I’ve never even seen his face! I don’t even know his name. He is a stranger.

I feel him reach beside me to pick up his belt. Unexpectedly, he slips it around my neck once more, forcing my head back towards him.

“You are fucking amazing, Raven. So. Fucking. Amazing.”

He trails his finger down my hip. When he pulls away, I instantly sadden at the familiar sounds of him dressing. How can I bear for him to do this to me over and over again? Better yet, how do I survive this in the end? I will be ruined. Who am I kidding? I am already ruined.

The door shuts behind me, and I know he is gone. Adjusting my skirt, I try to compose myself. I feel the warmth of his cum as it trails down my inner thigh. Reaching down, I swipe it with my finger and draw it into my mouth. The mixture of his pleasure and mine is so damn erotic, so delicious. I don't want to clean myself up. I want every part of him to remain on me. I wear his marking. He has claimed me. This man has awakened desires in me that I never want to sleep again.

Chapter Fifteen

Jaxxon

I can't wipe the smile off my face as I close the bathroom door behind me. Turning down the narrow corridor of the church, I hesitate at the table to take a mint from the crystal bowl. When I look up, two old ladies with horrified looks on their faces are standing in the hall. Judging by the looks on their faces, I'm sure they heard us in there fucking. Giving them a wink, I pop the mint in my mouth and continue walking.

I hear the gasping and loud talking as they both enter the bathroom. I'm sure Raven is about to get the scolding of her life, but I think she can handle them. People are so self-righteous. Sex is not something to be ashamed of. I bet the two old wenches haven't gotten any in years. I'll admit, fucking in a church is a bit much, but I would gladly chance losing my soul to experience that again with her. *Holy shit, that was off the charts HOT!*

My plan has worked. She's passed my test. I've reminded her who is in charge. The only catch is that I feel like I'm slipping even further out of control. She claims more and more of me each time I am with her. If things keep going like this, by the time this contract is over, I will be bowing at her feet. That can never happen. I will never love anyone.

Blaire

Throwing up my hand at the two women, I angrily fling open the door and leave. Something inside me has changed. I feel almost empowered by what we've just done. I feel no shame. I crave him and don't know why. He is a stranger; I know nothing about him.

I shouldn't be smiling, but I am. Being new to sex, I have nothing to compare this to, but I can easily say that this has been incredible. My body still hums from the excitement he made me feel. I don't know why, but every time we are together, I imagine Beautiful Man touching me. Maybe that is why I desire him so much. I've deluded myself with this fantasy.

Leaving the church, I head to the bank to make the wire transfer to the hospital. Afterwards, I grab a chicken salad sandwich from the corner deli and sit on the bench to enjoy the warm sunshine. People pass me by. Some men smile at me. I wonder if they know or can sense what I've just done.

Can they smell the sex that lingers on my body?

I close my eyes. I can still smell his cologne; his touch is saturated into my skin. When this contract is over, he will walk away; I will walk away.

Thing is, I am not sure I will want him to.

I'm not sure if I can.

Chapter Sixteen

Jaxxon

It's official. I'm a stalker.

I have told myself that I am not going to do it, but I've followed her home. This part of the neighborhood isn't bad, but the place where she lives should be condemned. The building looks as if it hasn't had any repairs in decades. This makes my blood boil with anger. I cross the street and make my way inside of her apartment building, scanning the list of tenant names on the inside mail boxes. My fingers land on the only Michaels name in the building. Michaels 4D. That has got to be her.

The elevator has an *OUT OF ORDER* sign taped to the outside. When I see an older lady with a walker having to take the stairs, it makes me want to find the owner and break his fucking legs. I gently take her arm and help her up the flight of stairs. As we reach her second level apartment, she pats me on the cheek and smiles. Once I leave her, I climb the additional two stories, and find myself standing in front of Blaire's apartment. Jiggling the doorknob, I am pissed to find it so loose. It doesn't take but one swipe of my credit card to gain access. As I look around the small, cramped space, I can't help but wonder how she lives here. The tiny living room is overtaken by a huge hospital bed and medical equipment. A small kitchen bar overflows with medicine bottles.

As I look around, I find myself drawn to the second door on the left. When I open the door, I am immediately slammed by her delicious scent. It's so damn hypnotic that it makes me lose myself for a moment. Closing my eyes, I slowly breathe in, savoring it as it flows deep into my senses. I open my eyes and take in the room around me. Her trophies, her awards, the framed snapshots of her life growing up, they all tell the story of my beautiful Blaire Michaels.

She deserves so much better than this place, so much more than the life that she's been handed. For the time being, Blaire belongs to me. And I intend to make things easier for her, starting right now.

Chapter Seventeen

Day 6

Blaire

The past two days have been a complete blur. Thankfully, my mom makes it through her surgery without any complications. The doctors have said they will have to watch for signs to make sure her body doesn't reject the valve they have placed in her. I think I've said at least a thousand prayers since they took her back for the procedure. Although she still hasn't woken up, the doctors are very pleased with her progress. Her color is already almost back to normal and the heat of her skin has finally returned.

Mr. R hasn't contacted me at all. I can't help but find that to be strange. I've even worried that something is wrong with my new phone, but that hasn't been the case. I can only assume that he will contact me when he is ready. Right now, I just need some rest. As much as I hate to, I'm going to have to return to my apartment to lay down. Maybe now that I know my mom's doing better, I can sleep more soundly in my own bed.

On the drive home, I can barely hold my head up. Parking the car across the street, I notice a huge moving van at the front entrance. Someone is either moving out of this dump or regretfully moving in. To be in a decent part of town, it is probably the most rundown building in the city. I don't know how it has managed to evade inspection like it does.

The Out of Order sign is no longer taped to the elevator door, and I'm left shaking my head in amazement. I've been living here for over a year now, and that thing stays broken more than it ever works. Normally, I would just as soon take the stairs, but I am so exhausted that I choose to take the ride on the elevator. I prop my head on the inside wall and listen for the fourth ding to indicate I've arrived on my floor.

As I step off the elevator, a heavyset man pushing a two-wheeler with boxes stacked high almost crashes into me.

"Oh, excuse me, Miss. I didn't see you," he politely apologizes.

"It's fine." I wave off our encounter and continue towards my apartment. Taking the few remaining steps, I rummage through my purse for my apartment keys. I am stunned when I reach my door and find it wide open.

For a second, I think it is just because I am so tired. I must be at the wrong apartment door. Then my eyes zone in on the picture frame in the mover's hand, and I know I am at the right place.

Wait! That's mine! What is going on?

"What the hell is going on?" I scream at the man covering my frame with bubble wrap. I reach down and snatch it out of his hands, and he frowns at me.

"We have orders to move this resident out of her apartment," the man says.

For a second, I panic. I haven't paid the rent yet for this month, but it is way too soon to be evicted.

Isn't it?

"Who are your orders from?" I demand and the large man huffs, shoving a clipboard into my clenched hands.

Scanning it over, the paperwork only shows my current address. It does not give any names for billing or who ordered the move in the first place. The only thing listed is the new address where they are moving me. This has got to be some sort of error. These men obviously have the wrong apartment.

"This is obviously a mistake. I'm not moving, so don't you

dare pack another thing!"

The heavyset man takes the clipboard from my hand and shakes his head at me.

"No mistake, ma'am. We were given specific orders to move everything from this address and set you up at the new address by this evening. If you don't mind, I need to keep on schedule."

"Now you listen here! This is my apartment and ..."

I am interrupted by the ringing of my designated phone.

Mr. R.

"Hello, Raven." His voice sends shivers through me.

"I am sorry, but this isn't a good time. I am dealing with something very import-"

He cuts me off before I can continue.

"Yes, well, important as it may be, need I remind you to not use that tone with me?"

"No, Sir, but you don't understand what is going on here."

"Tell me what is wrong, Raven. Why are you so upset? I don't like it."

"There are a whole team of movers here to move me out of my apartment. I can't get anyone to understand that this is some kind of mistake."

"It's no mistake, Raven. I issued the order myself."

"You? But why?"

"Where you live is unacceptable. I'm a very busy man, Raven, and I can't be worried about you when I am not around."

"Where I live is none of your business!" I yell into the phone. I try to disguise the hurt in my voice. Why is he putting down my home? He has no idea how hard I've fought to keep us here. The anger overtakes me, and I continue lashing out at him.

"I'm doing the best I can do! You don't understand anything about me! How could you?"

“Calm down, Raven.” His voice suddenly softens.

I have prepared myself to get a verbal lashing at my outburst with him. I’m sure I will be punished physically the next time he wants me.

“I’m trying to be calm, but you don’t understand what this is like for me. Especially right now,” I sob into the phone.

“I’m trying to help you, Raven, not hurt you. The place you were living was in such bad need of repairs that I couldn’t bear for you to live there another moment. I’m moving you somewhere where I know you will be safe and taken care of.”

“I appreciate your offer, but I can’t accept it. This may not be the Ritz to you, but it’s the best I can do for now.”

“The movers will move you to your new address, Raven. Your new place is completely furnished, but feel free to change anything you like with your things. I will be contacting you later this evening.”

And then the phone line goes dead. I stand there in a complete daze, looking at the phone in my hand. Movers continue moving around me, carefully packing items into boxes. Defeated, I stagger past them and go to my room, shutting the door behind me. Collapsing onto my bed, I no longer have the energy left in me to fight. Exhausted, I slowly begin to fall asleep. Beautiful man’s face is there when I close my eyes.

Jaxxon

Standing in my apartment, I stare out into the night. Car lights dance below and reflect across the dark river in front of me. No one would ever dispute that this is certainly the best view of the city. When I purchased this building three years ago, I renovated the top three floors, opening most of the space up like a studio apartment to appreciate the magnificent view through these large windows. Now, the new tenant below me can appreciate the same view she did when she signed her contract just days ago.

Yes, that's right. As of today, Blaire Michaels lives two floors below me. Whether she likes it or not, I will be taking care of her. Now that all the pieces of her puzzle come together, I'm seeing more and more about why she's so independent. She has been taking care of everyone else for quite some time now, and it's high time someone else starts taking care of her. She can fight me all she wants, but that is exactly what I will be doing.

Thanks to my doorman, I will always know her comings and goings. An earlier report indicated she has been here since the movers left. I've held off calling her all evening, trying to give her the space she needs to see that I did this all in her best interest. However, having her this close to me is a bit more than I originally bargained for. Even from two floors down, her body calls to me. My dick is throbbing to be back inside of her. Picking up my phone, I make the call to put myself out of my misery.

"Hello?" Her sleepy voice takes me back. I hadn't thought about how exhausted she must be from staying at the hospital with her mother.

"Raven. I hope you find your place acceptable." I switch my voice to firm. I can't let myself care. Nothing can stand in the way of getting what I want from her tonight.

"Yes, Sir, it is. Thank you."

Her response takes me back. I want her to fight with me. I don't want her to give in so easily.

"So, you aren't going to fight me anymore on this?"

"No, Sir." She sounds exhausted.

"Inside the top desk drawer in your living room is a key that will allow you access only to LEVEL 9 of this building. I've moved you closer to my playground, my pet. Now it is time to play."

"You are to come dressed to please, Raven. Don't disappoint me. You are to meet me there in twenty minutes. Remember, you are to wear your blindfold at all times."

"Yes, Sir."

I end the call. Throwing back my glass of whiskey, I smile at what I have in store for her tonight.

Tonight, my demon will play.

Chapter Eighteen

Blaire

By the time the movers leave the new apartment, I am aching and freezing. Pulling an extra cover over my body, I settle into my comfortable, new bed to try to get some rest. Maybe I can sleep whatever this is off and I'll feel better tomorrow. I've just barely gotten back to sleep when Mr. R calls my phone. I'm still pissed at him for demanding I move here, but a part of me can't help but be thankful. Either way, I am just too tired to fight him tonight.

When he insists I meet him tonight on an upper level of this place, I can't help but wonder why. Surely, he doesn't live here.

I stagger through the apartment, trying to dress. The room begins to spin, and my head is pounding. I need to freshen up, but there isn't time. Patting my hair down, I add some lip-gloss and make my way to the elevator. Following his instructions, I place the key into the hole beside LEVEL 9, and instantly, the elevator begins moving up. Tying the blindfold around my head, I prepare for the unknown.

I sense him the minute I hear the elevator doors open.

"Raven," he whispers and I nod in response. He takes my hand and leads me off the elevator.

When he lets go of me, I stagger forward, landing into his hard, thick chest. I'm shivering now.

"You're shaking, Raven. Don't be afraid. I'm not going to hurt you."

“I’m cold. So c- cold,” I say with my teeth chattering. I feel his hand on my forehead.

“Jesus! You are burning up!” He scoops me up into his arms. His warmth consumes me, and then darkness finds me. Briefly, I wake, aware that I’m being laid on a soft bed. I feel the silky comforter being pulled over me, and his warm hand brushing my hair away from my face. When my body continues shaking, he pulls me against him to warm me. I am too weak to move the blindfold away.

“I don’t need anyone taking care of me.” My voice is so weak.

“Rest,” he says, gently kissing my head.

“I am sorry. I–”

Sleep overtakes me.

Jaxxon

I lay here in her bed, holding her tightly against me. This is certainly not what I expected when I called her this evening. Once she’d drifted off to sleep, I carried her back downstairs to her apartment. The moment I placed her in her bed, she began shivering again. I couldn’t leave her that way, so I climbed into her bed and pulled her back against me. Little did I know what kind of impact that would have on me.

I’ve not done this before. I’ve never just laid in bed, holding another woman unless we were fucking. I never knew it could feel this way. It is so hard to have her this close to me, knowing that I can’t have her, but it feels so right that I never want to let her go.

She’s been sleeping now for over an hour, and in that time, I’ve managed to memorize every perfect thing about her face. I’ve even risked taking off her blindfold just so that I can stare at her.

The sweat forming on her brow relieves me. It means that her fever is finally going down. I look down at her and smile, tucking her dark lock of wavy hair away from her face. Sliding out of from behind her, I ease the covers back over her shoulders and place a kiss on her skin. Leaving her is hard as fuck, but I can't risk her waking up to find me here. Not yet, anyways.

Closing the door behind me, I let myself out of her apartment. As I ride the elevator back up the top floor, I am lost in thought. How is it that she owns so much of me already? If I don't end this soon, she will see what darkness lies inside. She will run. I can never let her see it. No one is allowed to see my demon.

Chapter Nineteen

Day 7

Blaire

I wake up later the next morning feeling disoriented. Was last night all a dream? The scent on my sheets tells me that it isn't. His delicious spicy cologne still lingers on my skin. The last thing I remember is stepping off the elevator. He must have carried me back up to my room after I fell asleep. I just hope he isn't upset with me about ruining his night.

After taking a long, hot shower, I quickly dress in a white denim skirt and light pink top. I feel rested and refreshed by the time I leave for the hospital. Thankfully, I am no longer running a fever and my appetite has returned. When I arrive at the hospital, I decide to not go into her room. I don't want to risk the possibility of giving her something since I had ran a fever last night.

Just as I turn to leave, Dr. Flannery makes his way down the hallway, talking to several other men in suits. My heart stops when I catch a closer glimpse at Beautiful Man walking beside him. Dressed in another crisp, tailored suit, he looks like a dream. His dark eyes lock with mine before they slowly travel down the length of my body, landing on my long, exposed legs. My face flushes, and I try to drop my head to hide my face.

No! No! This can't be happening! What if he recognizes me from dancing the other night? Shit! Of course, he recognizes me! The image of Honey on her knees, sucking his cock is burned in my brain. What am I going to do?

Dr. Flannery stops when he spots me standing there. I'm still paralyzed by the perfect man beside him. I imagine tearing off that suit of his and sucking his cock. I've thought about him every single time that Mr. R. touches me. This Beautiful Man is the only reason I have been able to do the things I've done. Imagining him doing all of the things to me makes my face blush and my pussy ache.

God, how I would love for this man to take me right here, right now!

"Ms. Michaels? Is everything alright?" Dr. Flannery jolts me out of my fantasy. I blink out of my daze and try to compose myself. For some reason, I have temporarily lost the ability to speak.

"Dr. Flannery!"

A nurse's frantic voice interrupts us.

"Oh, Blaire! Good. You're still here! Your mom is waking up!"

Forgetting everything, I dart back down the hallway and into my mom's room. The nurses are taking her vitals, but are smiling.

The moment I step in the room, she turns her head to the side and gives me a smile. Her beautiful green eyes sparkle against her glowing skin.

"Blaire, Baby?" she says and I run to her. I know I shouldn't be near her after being sick yesterday, but I need to touch my mom.

"Mom," I cry, tenderly wrapping my arms around her neck.

"Oh, Baby, don't cry. I'm gonna be just fine now."

"I thought I'd lost you. I have been so worried."

Dr. Flannery interrupts us and I turn to see several men standing there in the room behind me. Beautiful Man's eyes still look at me with a heated intense gaze. I swear the temperature in the room just shot up 30 degrees.

"Ms. Michaels, I am Dr. Flannery. We are pleased to see you

are finally awake," he says to my mom while reviewing the information the nurses just gave him.

"Your vitals look very good and it appears your surgery was successful. If all goes well, you should be able to go home in a few days."

His words are music to my ears. I don't bother to let her know that our home isn't home anymore. I will have to think of some good explanation for that one.

"I'd like for you to meet some of my business associates." He motions to the men in the room as he introduces them by name. I pay close attention to the way Beautiful Man is now fidgeting.

Why is he so nervous?

"And finally, this is Jaxxon Ryder, Vice President of Ryder Technology. His company is the one who sponsored your surgery." He introduces Beautiful Man to us.

What did he just say?

Jaxxon doesn't speak. He just nods his head and looks back to my mom.

Bolting out of the room, I make my way downstairs to the patient account department. Nothing about this makes any sense. I have got to get some answers now.

"Hello, dear, how are you today?" the older lady behind the desk asks me.

"I need to speak to someone about my mom's account. I just had money wired for her bill."

"Let me just look that up for you. It will only take a moment. Have a seat," she says, motioning for me to sit. She studies the screen for a few moments as she types a few keys here and there.

"Yes, I see where that electronic draft was re-deposited into your account. Your mother's bill is completely being taken care of by a private sponsor, it looks like."

Ryder Technology

How is it that, of all people, it would have to be him? I don't want him knowing anything about my life. I don't want him feeling sorry for me.

I don't give the woman a chance to continue. I have to get out of here. Hurriedly, I make my way to my car. My hands are shaking as I try to place the key into the ignition. Three times, I try to start it, all ending in nothing. The fourth attempt only makes it worse, resulting in a loud grinding noise followed by lots of smoke pouring out from beneath my hood. Every single light on my dashboard lights up and I can't help it. I scream! I punch. I shake the steering wheel in anger. When the smoke of my car simmers down, I see him. Jaxxon Ryder stands looking at me through the smoke in front of my car.

I'm embarrassed at how I had run out of the room earlier, but now, I am mortified. If anything, I should be getting out of my car to thank him for what his company has done for us.

I expect him to walk over and help me, but he doesn't. He just breaks our stare and keeps walking until he reaches a shiny black sports car. Once he is inside, he hauls ass out of the parking garage. Calling a tow truck, I have the car sent to the nearest garage. No one is able to look at it until tomorrow, so it is safe to say that I will be needing a rental. The greasy man at the garage promises that one will be delivered by this afternoon at my apartment.

Since I know Jaxxon has now left the hospital, I call a cab to take me back there. Right now, seeing my mom awake will be the only thing that keeps me from breaking.

The kind, old doorman opens my door when the cab pulls up to the apartment building entrance. I don't think I will ever get used to this.

"Good afternoon, Ms. Michaels. Your car was delivered just a bit ago."

"Hi, James. Thank you, but I told you to please call me Blaire."

"Yes, ma'am. I'll have to remember that," he says, winking at me.

I follow him back to his desk where he hands me a large, black vinyl folder. Inside is the manual to a brand new, black Lexus IS 350 F Sport convertible. An envelope is attached to the inside of the folder. Confused, I open it up, finding both the key and a note.

No rentals for my Raven. This is now yours. No arguments!

Mr. R

How did he know about this already? Is he following and spying on me everywhere I go? Do I have some sort of tracker device on me?

I stare down at the expensive car in front of me. I can't accept this! It is way too much.

I do something I should have done already today. I call to break my contract.

Jaxxon

Leaving her in the parking garage is beyond painful. I am not supposed to witness her weak moment. The way she looks as she unleashes her fury on the car tells me this is far more than about just it. I should keep walking, but instead, I stand frozen, captivated by her. When she finally looks up at me, her eyes are so desperate and pleading. And what do I do? I walk away. That's right. I turn and walk away. Coward. Asshole. Evil.

Each step, I grow angrier and angrier with myself. I barrel out of the parking lot, leaving her behind. What she doesn't know is that I never really left her. When the wrecker arrived, I followed her to the garage. Once she left the garage, I walked inside. She had been none the wiser.

That piece of shit of hers is scrap metal somewhere now. I should have done that a long fucking time ago. I've cancelled her rental and make one more stop on the way home. She will never worry about a broken down car again.

I have just gotten out of a meeting when she finally calls me. Already she is breaking the rules of the contract, but I have expected this call.

"Hello, Raven."

"I want out."

"Excuse me? I'm afraid that isn't possible."

"Yes, it is. I will return the money to you. I haven't spent any of it. I don't want the car, and I will see if I can still move back into my old apartment."

"First of all, you don't have a job, Raven. How exactly are you going to pay the rent?"

"How do you know I don't have a job anymore? Are you following me everywhere I go?"

"You don't have a job because I bought Club Climax. I kept Mike on as the manager, gave him a huge percentage to keep running the place, and demanded he let you go."

"How dare you! You can't do this to me."

"Dare? Oh, Sweetheart, it is you that doesn't want to dare me. And trust me, I do anything I damn well please. You of all people should know that."

"I will find another job. You can't buy out every place I work."

"I wouldn't be so certain of that, Raven."

"So the apartment building I lived in before, I suppose you bought that, too, right?"

"I suppose." I chuckle into the phone. I am loving this side of her. The rage and fearlessness in her voice is making me fucking hard as hell.

"You fucking bastard!"

I laugh at her words.

“Call me what you want, my dear. But for seven more days, you are mine. Unless of course, you prefer to be homeless, broke, and stranded without a car. ”

“I will never be yours!” she yells into the phone before hanging up on me.

Big mistake. Now I will have to show her who makes the rules.

Day 10

Blaire

It has been two days now since I hung up the phone on him. I thought I could forget him, but I can't. Everything has changed inside of me. I'm not that girl anymore. Blaire and Raven have perfectly blended now. I'm stronger than I've ever been because of him. I'm weaker now without him.

I need him.

I half expect him to come to my apartment and kidnap me. Part of me honestly fantasizes about it. My anger for him is erotic. My longing for him is desperate.

My mom is doing so much better. She should get to come home soon. Since she had been so weak before, they want to take extra precautions with her. I am grateful for that extra time. As messed up as my mind is right now, I don't know how good I would be to her.

Mr. R has ruined me.

I have just gotten home from the hospital when the phone he gave me begins ringing. I nearly break my neck getting to it on the kitchen bar.

Four rings.

Five rings.

Ten rings.

I don't answer it.

I can't.

He said he would never call me twice. Maybe now he will see that he doesn't overpower me.

An hour later, a knock startles me from reading a book. Since no one knows I even live here except Mr. R, I assume it is he. Looking through the peephole, I see a handsomely dressed man standing in front of my door. I recognize him as the manager of the building, Marcus Laux.

Nervously, I open the door.

Is he here to evict me?

I wouldn't put it past Mr. R.

"Ms. Michaels. I am sorry to disturb you, but we had a very urgent package delivered downstairs for you," he says, while handing me a sealed long, black envelope. I know exactly whom it's from.

"Thank you, Mr. Laux," I reply

"Goodnight, Ms. Michaels. If you need me for anything, please feel free to tell the doorman downstairs, and he will alert me immediately."

"Um, yes. Thank you, again," I manage to reply before closing the door. I still can't understand what this could be. Taking my finger, I ease it under the sealed flap in the back and tear open the back.

When I pull out the photos, I gasp. Picture after picture show me in all sorts of positions doing everything imaginable to an unidentifiable man.

Mr. R.

With trembling hands, I open the attached folded note.

I told you once to never underestimate me. You are mine for the next 4 days. Answer your goddamn phone or these might accidently be delivered to your mother.

He wouldn't dare!

Oh my God! Yes, he would!

My phone rings again, sending terror through me. I let the photos fall from my hand and rush to the phone.

Three rings. Four rings. I swallow the lump in my throat and answer it.

"H-ello."

"I see you received my package."

"How could you?"

"I think you know I can do anything I want. I felt the need to insure that you would fulfill your end of the bargain."

"But this is blackmail. I already told you I would give you everything back. I haven't even driven that car!"

"Do you think it is the money I want, my pet?"

"I don't know what you want any more. Whatever it is, I don't have it to give."

"Use the key, Raven. Level 9, now! You've kept me waiting long enough. Wear black lace."

The line goes dead. My heart sinks. My heart soars.

I have no choice. I want no other choice.

Chapter Twenty-One

Jaxxon

I'm in control.

Repeatedly, I say this to myself, but no matter how many times I do, I can't get it to sink in my head. I need her to be reminded of this. Hell, who am I kidding? I am the one that needs reminding of it. Tonight, I will test her limits and push her far past them. I can't allow her a choice in the matter. I'm doing all of this… well, simply because I can.

I turn up my glass and take a swig of my whiskey while I watch her on the monitor. Moving the controls, I focus in closer on her face.

My beautiful Raven. My beautiful Blaire.

I lightly trace my fingertips over the large monitor screen where her mouth is.

So goddamn gorgeous.

My cock begins throbbing at the memory of those plump luscious lips wrapped tightly around it. I feel the intense pressure of my dick as it presses harder against the zipper of my jeans.

Adjusting myself, I slip off my shirt and toss it to the side. Taking another drink, I smile at how delicious she looks sitting in that chair blindfolded. Truthfully, it could have been taken off a long time ago, but it gives me a thrill like no other to remain anonymous. When I fuck her, I know she craves Jaxxon. Little does she know, it's actually he that is fucking her. But I need her eyes covered. I don't want her to see the evil that lives within me. I'm in too deep now. I can't bear her running away.

Level 9.

This floor of my building has been designed to my exact specifications. Most workers on this renovation thought this would be a luxury, personal gym. Honestly, I guess in a way it is, since I always get quite the work out in here with my submissives.

To avoid anything in my lifestyle being leaked to the public, I have assembled all of my equipment myself. My family's pristine reputation could never survive if people find out what I do behind closed doors. That is why ALL my submissives wear blindfolds. No exceptions. I can't risk the consequences if they ever find out who I am.

Level 10

The only ones who don't wear the blindfold are the girls I just fuck and leave in a hotel room. No one has ever slept in my bed. Actually, no woman other than my housekeeper has ever been to my penthouse on Level 10. I've never awakened next to a woman. I live by the rule: *FUCK AND LEAVE – DON'T BRING HOME.*

The world already looks at me as the irresponsible playboy with all of the countless women I've been with. But I am who I am. I own it with no shame. I have fucked some HOT ones over the years. But absolutely no one compares to Blaire, not even close.

She doesn't know it, but I got that damn contract off the internet. Hell, I only added a few parts in it to scare her, but it isn't as if it would ever be brought to a legal person or anything. She is naive to believe I ever actually would. I've never contracted any of my submissives in the past. They are all contracted anonymously and brought here to me by my driver who makes them use the blindfold for complete discretion. Money is no object to me. I've found the more I pay, the more I got to play. The demon inside me loves to play hard.

I like variety, choosing to stick to the same one only a couple of times before moving on to sample another. Boring easily, I always get my fill early on. The thing is, I will never bore of her. She intrigues me more and more every single day. I will never get enough of this girl. She is burrowed into my soul now. I should claw her out of it, but then I would have nothing. Not that I had much to begin with.

I can take no more. My demon needs her. I need her.

It is time.

Sitting down my glass, I exit the room and walk across the hallway to where Raven is waiting. She jumps when I close the door behind me, and I breathe in her fear. Call me a sick bastard, but I get a fucking high on it.

God! That smell of her terror is fucking fantastic.

I revel in it, allowing my demon to feast upon all of it. She sits with her back facing me in a narrow chair. The wooden backing has wide slats that expose her toned, elegant back to me. I hiss at the sight of the black lace bra that she wore at my request.

Good girl!

I walk behind her and place my hands on her trembling shoulders. Her skin is like warm silk against my hands. I should stop there, but I feel the need to comfort her, so I gently stroke down her arms. She relaxes against the chair and leans her head back seeming to enjoy my touch. I lift her hand and caress the skin around her wrist before gently placing a kiss on it. She melts again. Quickly, I let go.

This isn't for her. It is for me, I remind myself.

Removing the zip ties from my pocket, I secure them around her arm and then to the wooden back of the chair. She begins writhing in panic. Violently, I grab a fistful of her hair and pull it back. Her lips tremble. I lean over her and lick them with my tongue.

The demon within speaks.

"Don't fucking move," I warn her, my voice harsh and uncaring. A pang of regret hits me and angers me.

I must hold back.

"Tell me your safe word, Raven."

"Snowflake," she says, her voice raspy and sexy. My cock twitches at the delicate word she's chosen. Fuck me! Why did she have to pick that word? It makes me want to be rougher with her. I will stop at nothing to make her see just how much of me she can stand. I want that word screamed from her lips.

The demon demands it. I desperately need it.

Releasing her hair, I move to her front. The bottom of this chair slides up and out, releasing a spreader bar. I anchor her feet to the sides of the bar, and then zip tie her ankles to the bottom of the chair. I could use the metal shackles, but I want to see the marks I leave on her skin. She needs them to remind her. I need her to see them. I can smell her delicious cunt, and it is driving me insane with need. I have to get out of her now before I throw this whole plan out the door and fuck her.

Panting, I frantically make my way back inside the control room. She sits there, turning her head from side to side, hoping to get a clue as to what is going on. Her chest quickly rises and falls repeatedly.

Good girl! Be scared of the demon.

I press a button on my panel and begin playing random sounds in the room. A thunderous crash has her jumping and shaking against her restraints. She withers more, shaking her head as I repeat it over and over, rotating it in the speakers around her. I add another of loud glass crashing. And then I leave her in silence. When her chest slows, I repeat the process again. Her fear and terror makes me prideful inside. I feed the evil within. Again, she tries to wiggle out of the chair, but it does no good. Her fears are peaked, and I love every moment as I study her face closely on the monitor.

It is time. She is ready.

"It is time to show the girl pleasure. Don't hold anything back from her," I order through the speaker of another room.

Seconds later, the door to the room opens and I see Raven twisting in the chair. I watch it all play out in front of me on the large 72" monitor on the wall. Another stab of guilt overtakes me, and I fight to clear it from my thoughts. Nothing can get in my way of doing this.

"It's show time."

Blaire

Except for almost losing my mom, I've never been more scared in my life. I don't know if I can do this, and I need to. I have to. I can't risk losing this money. I feel helpless and vulnerable like this. I can't see anything, and now I am restrained and exposed. It is thrilling in a way, but terrifying as hell.

He has been so rough with me. Each time he touches me, electricity soars through my body. My sex is dripping with pleasure from when he pulled my hair.

Why is my body responding to him like this? This can't be normal. Something is wrong with me.

Random sounds fill the room, confusing me.

What's going on? What is that? Oh, God!

A loud boom erupts around me followed by glass shattering. I jump and turn my head. I can't move, and being blindfolded makes my senses almost superhuman. I am terrified. He's being mean now, and I want him to stop. He has promised not to hurt me, and I believe what he has said. It's just that I have a limit that I can take. I have my safe word. He knows it now, but I don't want to ever have to use it. I don't want him to break me. I don't think it is even possible to break what is already broken and not worth fixing. I'm afraid that if I ever use the word, this contract will be over. If that happens, I will not be able to pay back the money that he has fronted me.

Everything has grown quiet now.

Much too quiet.

The door behind me opens and closes.

He is back.

The minute I hear the footstep, I know it isn't him. The familiar clicking sound of stilettos reveals that it belongs to a female. Why is there a woman in here with me? Realization hits me, paralyzing every inch of my body.

Oh, God! No! Please! NO!

I know that I'm not allowed to speak, so I bite down onto my bottom lip, holding the fear inside. Lightly, a fingertip traces my face and trickles down my jaw. I feel her leg slide across mine as she positions herself to straddle me. I instantly turn my head away in disgust when I feel her lean into me. Her heavy, hot breath against my lips is making me sick. I think she is trying to kiss me.

I don't want this. NO!

Suddenly, her tongue grazes the lip that I'd damn near bit off. Her hands move to cup my face. Protesting furiously, I shake my head back and forth, trying to get her to stop. But she doesn't. Her hands slide down my chest and capture my breasts. She vigorously squeezes my nipples through my sheer bra, twisting them upwards as she grinds her core against me. Hot tears fill my eyes.

Please, make her stop. I don't want this.

My body is shaking uncontrollably. I try to take deep breaths, but I can't control it.

Damn him for this! Damn everything about my fucking life!

The girl leans in again and grabs my face, turning it to the side as she leans in to speak.

"Relax, Raven. It's me." Honey's voice fills my ear.

NO! He can't ask this of me!

I go to speak, but she clamps her hand over my mouth.

"Don't speak. We both need this money, so don't ruin

anything. Just relax and go with it. He asked me to be gentle with you."

She kisses me, and I shake my head the whole time in protest. I want her off of me. Her tongue moves down my neck while her hand moves down my abdomen. I try like hell to squeeze my thighs together, but it is useless. My legs are locked wide open in some sort of device at my feet. Every time I move, some sort of plastic digs deeper into my skin, marking me of this terror.

She further extends my torture by inching her arm further and further downward. Fighting her with all my might, I twist and shake my head, bucking in my chair, anything that will make her stop.

"Stop it, Raven!" she yells at me and then violently yanks my hair.

"I need this money. Don't you dare fuck it up for me!"

She begins again, this time more forcefully holding my front down with her weight. I feel everything leaving me. I want to scream out my safe word, but I can't. Everything is slowing down around me. Please, Lord, make it stop.

I try switching to Raven, but she has given up. Blaire remains awake in me, and she can't take anymore either. The fight leaves my body.

Becoming numb, I no longer struggle. I no longer care. The word is on the tip of my tongue to end it. My body releases the tension as my mind snaps.

Chapter Twenty-Two

Jaxxon

I watch the whole thing in complete horror.

What have I done?

I thought this would push her beyond her limits and make her yield more to me. I wanted her to see who was in control. I never expected this to break her. Normally, I'd love to fuck two girls, but that was never the intent for tonight anyways.

"SAY IT!" I scream at the monitor in front of me. Watching her lips, I am begging her to say that one word so that I can stop all of this. She fights, but she doesn't speak.

"Just fucking say it!" I yell, throwing the bottle of whiskey against the wall. I am so pissed at myself, and I hate that I'm feeling this way!

And then I witness her body go completely limp, making her slouch in the chair. Her head hangs down, allowing her gorgeous dark waves to shield her face. She is no longer shaking. She is no longer fighting.

NO!

Throwing a black ski mask over my face in disguise, I run out of the room. They are only across the hall from me, but I can't seem to get there fast enough. Slamming back the door, I waste no time pulling Honey off of Raven.

"Get the fuck out!" I scream at her. My eyes zone in on Raven and I rush to where she is. Sheer panic overtakes me as I grasp her head to lift it up to me. Brushing her curls away from her face, I struggle with removing her blindfold. I need her to be all right. My heart drops to my stomach. I lean in closer.

"Raven? Raven!" I whisper across her lips. I taste her tears and close my eyes. I turn all my hatred toward Honey who is still standing behind me.

"I said GET OUT! You'll still get your money. Go back into the other room. Someone will come and take you home. Now leave!"

"Is she all right?" Honey asks, concerned as she clenches the door handle in her hand for dear life.

"JUST FUCKING GO!" I scream again and she finally leaves us alone.

I slam down the lock behind her and frantically remove my ski mask.

Removing the utility knife from the drawer next to me, I hurriedly begin setting her free. Her wrists are raw and tinged bright red from bleeding. Moving to her feet, I cut the plastic off and free her from the bar. She still hasn't moved or responded.

What have I done?

Pulling her forward, I gently scoop her into my arms. Cradling her against me, I fall to the floor.

"Raven," I whisper in her ear, moving my hands to remove the blindfold. I don't want her to see who I am, but I can't bear to leave her like this. The moment I touch the black lace, she immediately pushes off of me. Her enormous gasp of air strangles her. Shaking her head, she desperately climbs backwards away from me and readjusts the lace on her eyes. The fear on her face is sickening.

"S-Snowflake! SNOWFLAKE!" she screams and pushes her hands out in front of her, warning me to back off.

That word guts me, tears my soul in half. It's the sharpest pain, the hardest blow I've ever experienced, all rolled in one.

Before now, I had maliciously plotted for her to break down to say it. Now, I never want to hear that word ever again.

I want to cut the demon inside of me out. Allow him to hemorrhage on the floor in front of me.

"How could you do that to me? And why did you have to pick her? Why?" she sobs, pulling herself to her body to hide.

I lunge forward, grabbing her flailing hands and pulling her into my arms. "Raven, I'm so sorry," I whisper against her lips. The need to be with her is so intense that I can't bear it any longer.

I have to make this right!

Cupping her face, I crush my lips to hers and swallow her muffled cries. She melts against me, wrapping her arms around my neck, pulling me in closer. Our hunger is fierce; our desire is unimaginable. Rolling her to her back, I work my kisses down her neck, stopping to savor the smooth skin near her shoulder. Forcefully, I pull the satin bra strap down and move down to engulf her full breast that escapes.

Biting down hard on her nipple, I press my hardness to her warm core. I can feel how drenched she is through my jeans.

Growling in response, I flip us, pulling her on top of me. Reaching around to her back, I unclasp her bra and throw it behind me. Her breasts fall free, and she immediately shields them in embarrassment. I pull her arms to me and bite her jaw, raking her neck hard with my teeth as I trail them to her ear.

"Don't ever hide from me, Baby. You are so fucking stunning."

Her hips move and I feel like my cock is going to break from the pressure against these pants.

Rolling her once more to her back, I reach down and unbutton my jeans. Her innocent hands hesitate at first, but then she grasps the waistband to begin tugging them down. They only reach below my ass before my throbbing cock pops free. I can feel her heat calling for my starving dick. I want to taste her, savor her, but I need to be in here now. With one hard thrust forward, I enter

Heaven. Slowly, I pull out and then slam back into her.

Jesus Christ! Nothing has ever been as good as being with her!

Once more, I pull out, but this time, I ease myself back inside of her. The sensation is so magnificent that it makes my eyes roll back into my head. For a second, I forget everything around me. Just as I am about to explode all in her, I feel her hands on my bare backside, urging me on. I breathe in deep, trying to calm myself a bit before continuing.

Her hips waver beneath me. Her intense hunger ignites me. Losing all sense of control, I impale her with my thick cock and steady my pace. Her nails dig into my hips, and I increase the intensity of my thrusts. Holding myself up with one arm, I sweep the hair away from her face with my free hand. I'm definitely not going to last long. Lifting up, I reach beneath her and pull her perfect, plump ass in with my hands, forcing her take all of me.

She feels so fucking good.

"Fuck! Baby, you feel so damn good. Tight."

She bites her lip to hold in her pleasure, and I engulf her mouth once more with a long, deep, passionate kiss. I don't want her to hold back. I want her to drown my cock with her cum.

"I want to hear you scream, Raven. Let go. Come with me," I order her, and she automatically yields to my demands. Her pussy clamps down around my cock, and I struggle to hold my release back until she is there with me.

"Oh! YES! Aghhh!" she screams and then I feel her come hard on my dick. That is all it takes to set me over the edge.

"I'm going fill that sweet pussy up with my cum! Fuck yes!" I follow her, screaming my own release as I pound into her. Collapsing against her chest, I struggle to pull my eyes from the back of my head.

My throbbing cock is still hard and ready. I need more of her. I push myself up and try to catch my breath. Leaning in, I tenderly kiss her lips as I slide out of her. I move further down, feathering kisses on her flat toned stomach, working my way down to my destination. When I reach her mound, I pause and move to her inner thigh.

She is drenched in both of our juices, and the delicious smells of sweet sex invade my nose. Licking inward, I savor our flavors on my tongue. Her body shakes as I move to that sweet clit of hers. Swiping my tongue upwards, I lick her clean as I suck her clit in hard against my teeth.

I smile when I feel her hands in my thick hair.

"I'm nowhere near done with you, Raven."

Thrusting in and out with my tongue, I work her pussy hard. Cupping her ass cheeks in my hand, I feel her lose control in my arms. Her pussy drenches my mouth with her release. I drink it all down and crave even more. Moving over her body, I kiss her lovingly, allowing her to taste herself. She smiles, and I growl with desire, flipping her over and positioning her on all fours. Pulling her hips back to me, I line up my cock to her glistening opening. I admire how perfect and beautiful her luscious pink folds are.

I swear to God, every inch of this woman is gorgeous as fuck!

Giving myself a few pumping strokes, I marvel at the gorgeous sight of her glorious ass up in the air. Rubbing her ass cheek, I lean forward and enter her. Normally when I take women from behind, it is hard and quick, but not this time. Slow and easy is something I have never done before her. Firmly gripping her hips, I ease myself into her, going deeper than I ever have before.

Sweet Jesus!

The sensation is fiercely incredible and I find myself rolling my eyes back again at the feeling of being in her like this.

"Shit! Raven, I can't get enough of you," I whisper against her ear.

She rocks her hips against my dick and I push down hard on her ass.

"Let go! Give it to me, Raven! Don't hold it in!"

"Oh. My. God!" she screams and I keep my slow pace. Her

inner walls squeeze my dick once more, milking me into a screaming climax.

"Yes that's right! Yeah, Baby! Fuck that cock! AGHH!" I roar.

She falls forward, and I stagger behind her, catching myself before I collapse on top of her. Kissing her lightly on her back, I step away from where she is. I don't know what is going on with me, but this means far more than I ever realized it would. She means more to me than I could ever possibly imagine.

She is mine.

Looking at her once more, I can't help myself. I lean down and kiss her on the top of her head.

"Don't move."

I walk into the nearby bathroom, run warm water over a soft white washcloth, and return to her. Dropping back down to my knees, I gently begin washing her. Taking a blanket down from above us, I wrap her up and lift her into my arms. Gently, I deposit her on the nearby bed in the room. Pulling her up against me, I trace the lines of her shoulder as she relaxes into me.

"Tell me about yourself," I ask her. Maybe I don't deserve to know, but I crave it.

"There isn't much to tell. I'm not that interesting."

My beautiful Blaire, if you only knew.

"Tell me everything," I reply.

For the next few hours, I hang on to her every word. No story could ever be more intriguing.

There is no use fighting this. I am falling deep for her.

Chapter Twenty-Three

Day 11

Jaxxon

She consumes me. Every minute of every day, she owns more of me. She's in every thought, in every dream. I cannot escape her control. I feel as if I need her for my next breath. The fear of losing her is unfathomable. How is it that, in such a short amount of time, I've found myself surrendering to a woman?

It is late in the evening and I have been dealing with paperwork all day. I need to finish getting everything together in order to be able to brief the board on how well our patient, Ms. Michaels, is doing. Tomorrow morning, I will be meeting her to discuss my businesses involvement with her case. No matter how hard I try, I haven't been able to get anything done for thinking about last night with Blaire.

Why did I have to stay?

Why did I insist on getting to know her more?

Why had I moved her fucking two floors beneath me?

Until last night, I'd convinced myself that our attraction had been merely physical and sexual. I'd been very wrong.

We share an emotional and spiritual connection as well.

I am hopeless now.

Stacy twists into my office, radiating confidence and projecting her uncanny desire for me. Her heavy tits bounce with each stride, threatening to spill out of her tight, red, low cut sweater. The short black skirt she is wearing is definitely not work appropriate attire, but nothing has ever been appropriate about Stacy. She'd never been anything but an easy fuck to me. Even though her body screams perfection, something about her has always bored me. Being with her never completely satisfies me.

She shuts the door behind her, locking the top lever. Seductively, she moves toward me, unbuttoning the front of her red sweater as she inches closer. I don't stop her. Instead, I lean back in my chair and enjoy the show. Yes indeed! This is exactly what I need. Fucking Stacy will get Blaire out of my mind and remind me of who I really am. I've let a woman overpower me and that simply can't happen.

Stacy drops her sweater on the floor beside my desk and leans forward, grabbing the armrests on my chair. Her red lace bra barely manages to hold her breasts inside. Licking my lips, I can taste them already. She straddles me in my chair and reaches around to remove her bra. I waste no time engulfing her breast in my mouth. Stacy throws her head back and moans. Blaire's face immediately comes to mind, and I suck harder on her erect nipple. She grinds herself against my hardness while frantically working my belt loose. Panting, she stands and drops to her knees, slowly sliding my pants zipper open and allowing my cock to spring free.

I lift up off my seat as she slides my pants down. Cupping my balls with her hand, she grabs my throbbing cock and begins pumping me up and down.

"I knew you'd missed me. Let me give you what you need." Her voice echoes in my office.

I don't open my eyes. I can't. I need to do this.

Her hand pumps faster and faster. I lean further back, allowing her to pull harder on my cock. I need to fuck her now! I feel her hot breath as it approaches her destination. Her hot tongue runs up my long shaft while her other hand continues squeezing my balls. Hearing her intake of breath, I know she is about to take me into her mouth. All I can see is Blaire. Fisting her hair into my hand, I want Blaire. Then I make the ultimate mistake.

I open my eyes.

She's not Blaire.

Stacy looks up at me and winks just as she is about to take my cock into her mouth. Disgust fills my stomach at what I am doing. Full of regret, I instantly shove her off me.

"Get out!" I scream at her, pulling up my pants and securing my belt.

Stacy gets up off the floor and angrily grabs her things, heading to the bathroom in my office. Clutching her clothes to her body, she turns to me and snarls.

"You fucking asshole! You're going to wish you never did that!" she yells, slamming the bathroom door behind her.

I don't give her a second chance to scold me. Grabbing my jacket and keys, I bolt from my office with one thing on my mind. Showing Blaire Michaels just who is boss.

Blaire

I'd barely made it to the new apartment when my phone vibrates.

Mr. R: Level 9 NOW!

Fear overtakes me. He is angry.

Why?

I thought we had worked through this. He is all I've thought about today.

I press my key inside the panel, and the elevator begins the journey up to the 9th level. Securing the silk around my head, I hear the doors open in front of me.

I feel him immediately as his energy penetrates my soul. And then everything in my world snaps. His large hands grab for my neck, shoving me back hard into the elevator wall.

"What are you trying to do to me?" he growls in my ear.

I am paralyzed in confusion.

What does he mean?

"I don't understand," I manage to answer him with a strangled voice.

His grip tightens around me; his hot breath in my ear makes me dripping wet for him.

"You care about me, don't you? Damn it, Raven! That's not part of the agreement," he snarls at me.

"Sometimes we can't control how we feel."

He drops his hand from my throat and hits the elevator wall beside me. I feel the force of the blow as the wall vibrates behind me. Had he wanted to hit me?

He thinks he is evil, but he isn't. I have felt the way he holds me. I know he cares about me, too. Why can't he admit he feels something for me?

"I want you to show me your darkness. Let me be your light."

"You've awakened the demon inside of me. You need to run while you still can."

"I don't want to run. I want you to free your demon. I am not afraid."

"You should be very afraid, Raven."

"I will never be afraid of you, Sir."

"Raven… don't," he whispers against my lips. His body trembles as he holds me in his grasp for dear life.

"Show me," I whisper into his mouth.

He draws in a deep breath, and then with one violent rip, he tears off my wrap dress, sending buttons flying all around us. Forcefully, he grabs a fistful of my hair, and drags me out of the elevator. His breathing is ragged, his pace frantic with direct purpose.

Oh my God! What have I done? Can I do this? I've never seen him this angry before.

The metal blade slides against my skin and then a loud clip sounds as my bra is cut from my body. Moving downward, one jerk rips my thong from my hips, leaving me completely naked and exposed to him. I have nothing more I can hide behind.

"The demon is ready to play." He growls.

Chapter Twenty-Four

Blaire

With a handful of my hair in his hands, he forces me forward onto the platform, causing me to trip over my feet. I've pushed him to this madness. I'm the one who called out the inner demon inside of him. I want him to see that I need this just as much as he does. I want him to make me forget everything; this is all I want to feel. He needs to see that I am not running away. The pain he awards me is my pleasure. I welcome his harshness. I welcome his darkness. I'm in love with his demon.

My face slams against one of the cold thick wooden beams of the cross. My flat stomach rests upon the cool metal that connects the middle piece of the X. His heavy weight prevents me from moving. His face presses into the back of my hair. He breathes me in and then raises my hands one by one above my head, securing them to the beams. He presses his hardness into my ass, and I can't help but press back into him. His hand pushes my head to the side away from the wood. His foot violently kicks my bare ankles apart. It only takes him a second to snap the cold metal shackles around them. I am now his prisoner.

My skin burns from the abrasive rope he ties tightly around my waist. Looping between each leg, he wraps layer after layer around my thighs. Each twist of my body magnifies the burning sensation and taunts the pleasure between my thighs that is pleading to be released.

"Open!" he orders as he shoves a ball gag into my mouth and fastens it behind my head. When he pulls tightly on the leather strap, I scream in protest, which causes me to choke on my own spit. He backs away, leaving me gagged, tied, and blindfolded. I love every torturous second of it. Leather strands of a flogger gently slap against my back, sending my clit pounding. Mr. R. trails the leather up between my legs, hesitating at my pussy. Without warning, he slaps the flogger hard over and over onto my moist swollen opening. I'm lost in the pleasure surging through my body. I'm lost in him.

He stops and the warmth of his body leaves mine as he backs away.

I stand this way for what seems to be an eternity.

Five hard blows from what feels like a crop are delivered to my back, knocking the breath out of me. Still, I want more. I hold in my screams. I won't give him the satisfaction of knowing I love it. I know he wants me to beg, but that isn't going to happen.

Mr. R's hand softly caresses my ass. His fingertips tenderly inch up my side. The heat of his breath on the back of my neck is sending me closer to oblivion.

"I'm going to fuck you so hard that your pretty pink pussy is going to be black and blue when I am done pounding my dick inside of it."

I gasp for air when I strangle on my fear. I revel in the delight of the pain I crave. I never would have believed I would need this. All this time, I thought I wanted to keep control in my life, but the thing is I needed someone to control me. I needed someone to save me.

Unleash the demon. I am ready.

I push my ass out to him, teasing him as I sway it from left to right. Mr. R's breath halts as he sucks in another round of air. My backside is rewarded with an additional five hard blows. Suddenly, I feel him spit on my back. When he roughly spreads my cheeks, his warm spit reaches my openings. His nose trails up my pussy, inhaling me as he travels upward.

Breathing me in, he growls loudly. His searing, hot tongue impales my asshole with vengeance. He vigorously works the spit into my clit with his thumb. Then, two strong fingers ram into me, moving in a come-hither motion, catching the sensitive edges of my inner walls. My folds clamp down hard around him. He adds another finger and increases his movements inside of me, reaching deeper and deeper. The combination of his tongue in my ass and his fingers in my pussy spiral me to a new level of ecstasy. One, that before now, I'd have never thought conceivable. I bite down hard on the ball in my mouth.

He slides himself in my pussy and then unleashes the fucking he'd promised. Each hard thrust sends my head forward and my body sandwiches between him and the cross. I can't catch my breath. My release builds rapidly down low, begging to be set free. I'm almost ready to explode, but then he frantically pulls out of me, slapping me hard on the ass.

Then, like a light switch, he turns tender by caressing the warm red skin on my bottom. Sweetly, he leans over me, pulling back my hair from my face. Little did I know, his words would be anything but sweet.

"I'm going to claim this glorious ass, and you are not going to stop me. Scream all you want, but you WILL give everything to me. I am going to mark you as mine. I will take what has never been taken."

Oh God help me!

Jaxxon

I've lost all control. The demon inside me has taken over. Spitting once again, I watch my saliva pool around her asshole. I don't want to hurt her, but then again, I do. I am a sick bastard, but I want all of her whether her body is ready for it or not. Time should be taken with this demand, but I've thrown patience out the window. She's sent me over the edge tonight. I can't back down now. I've never needed something so much in all of my life. She is the only one to feed my inner demon's hunger. With her, its appetite is endless.

Rolling around my finger at the opening of her anus, I push apart her butt cheeks and watch her tiny bud open for me. Fresh and untaken, a beautiful, tight virgin ass. FUCK! I swirl my fingertip around her asshole and slide two fingers inside of her. Her moans are muffled by the ball gag in her mouth. I pump my long shaft with my free hand. Watching her writhe, I can take no more.

Ready or not, she is getting this now.

I step behind her, skin on skin. The little minx pushes her ass to me and sashays it from left to right. My fingernails dig into the flesh of her delectable hips and I lose the last bit of self-control I have left. As hard as I can, I impale her. She screams. I ram in harder. The cross shakes so hard that I'm convinced I am going to either break it or rip her arms off. I don't care. The metal digs deep into her skin. I wrap my arm around her stomach, pulling her closer to me. I can't get close enough. I want to crawl into her soul and consume it. I want to corrupt her. I want to pound her ass so hard she never stops screaming my name.

My name. She doesn't even know my fucking name. I want to hear Jaxxon on her lips. Will that ever happen?

I grow increasingly angrier at my own mistakes. I should have never agreed to keep my identity a secret. She should be staring in my eyes when I coat her in my seed. I have ruined that just as I ruin everything. Channeling my rage into my thrusting, I become beyond animalistic. My grunts are feral, my need insatiable. Her body should be revolted by my sick actions, but instead her ass grips a hold of my dick like a vice, milking me for my impending explosion.

She meets my thrusts; I dig my fingernails deeper into her skin. Her screams erupt the room, her body shakes with its release. I see the blood on my hands from where I've broken her skin. It sends me over the edge, rocketing me into a climax unlike any other I've experienced in my life. I feel the hot spurts of my semen shooting out as they coat her ass. Exhausted, I collapse against her. I feel the intensity of our connection. This is beyond powerful; this is something I never want to be without. There is no way I will ever let go of her.

The thick stream of my semen follows as I regretfully pull out of her. I instantly grieve the loss of her warmth around me. My cock rests against my leg, still erect and wanting more. Needing more. I smile and shake her ass, smearing the small streaks of blood into her skin. She is mine; I have officially claimed every inch of her now.

Chapter Twenty-Five

Day 12

Blaire

Two days.

All I have left is two days with him. I don't want our time to end and I don't know what will happen to me once it does. When there is nothing to hold over me, will he still want me? Will I still want him?

Of course, I will. I am in love with him. Love? Yes, I love him. I know nothing about him. I've never even laid eyes on him, but I love him. So just how fucked up does that make me? And what in the hell am I supposed to do about it?

Obviously, I can't tell him. He will think I am some desperate crazy woman. Men like him don't love anything but themselves. Even though I feel he cares about me in some way, something makes me believe he cares for me, but I should have known with a man like him that I'm nothing more than a possession. Simply said, I'm just a shiny new toy that he's no doubt grown tired of and now wants to move on to another.

No.

My stomach violently twists and turns in agony.

Another one.

What if he is already looking to replace me after our contract is up? The thought of him fucking someone else rip my heart in two. My stomach wrenches again at the thought and I barely make it to the bathroom in enough time to throw up.

These are going to be the longest and most torturous two days of my life.

Jaxxon

She is so stunning. I can't help but admire her from afar. Standing in the side hall, I watch as Blaire kisses her mother goodbye and leaves. I know her routine quite well by now. She arrives here around 8am and leaves around lunchtime to volunteer on the pediatric floor. Every day from 12:30pm—1:00 pm you can find her reading books, coloring, finger painting, or playing dolls with the sick kids on the floor. The kids adore her. I understand completely. I adore her, too. I like kids a lot. I have just never given much thought of having any. Not until her, anyways. She has shaken me to the core, opening my eyes to see a life I never thought possible.

She's done the impossible. She taught me to love.

Blaire Michaels has brought sunshine into my fucked up dark world, but that sunshine can't last forever. It only lasts for two more days. Then the luminous, dark cloud that has hovered over my life will return. Even though he remains quieter these days, the demon inside me still lives. She doesn't deserve to be with someone as screwed up as me. Blaire deserves a happily ever after with someone that won't corrupt her. In just the past ten days, I've felt I've done just that.

"Good afternoon, Ms. Michaels" I say as I knock lightly on her mother's hospital room door.

She beams me a smile as bright and contagious as her daughter. With her dark, wavy hair framing her youthful face, I can see so much of where Blaire gets her looks. Her twinkling green eyes are inviting and calm. Just like her daughter.

"Oh, please come in, Mr. Ryder. It's so good to see you!"

When I hand her the huge vase of colorful tropical flowers, her smile grows even wider.

"Oh my goodness. They are so beautiful!"

Just like your daughter.

"Thank you so much! These are my daughter's favorite."

Blaire. My Blaire. I will order her a room full.

"You are very welcome. How are you feeling?"

"So much better. I'll be even better once I get back home. My daughter has been working so hard to get everything ready for me. She even moved us into another place. One where the elevator actually works," she says, laughing. A pang hits me. I hate they've had to struggle so much.

Blaire.

"Well, I know you need your rest, so I won't bother you. Ryder Technology wanted to check in to see how you are doing."

"Please, Mr. Ryder, have a seat."

Hesitantly, I sit down in the chair next to her. Glancing nervously at my watch, I know I don't have long before she returns.

"Mr. Ryder, I just want to thank you for everything you have done for me. The past couple of years have been a real struggle for me, and unfortunately for my daughter, too."

"I'm sorry to hear that. Maybe now things will be better for you both."

"Mr. Ryder, if it weren't for your company's generosity, I would never have been able to get this surgery. My daughter has worked so hard at her night job trying to save enough money. But no matter how hard she has worked and saved, there just never is enough money. My Blaire is so young and beautiful; she shouldn't have had to quit school to come home to take care of me."

My sweet Blaire. I am so sorry. I didn't know.

"She sounds like an incredible woman. I know you must be

proud of her."

"I'm more than proud of that girl, Mr. Ryder. I just hope this will give us both a fresh start. Maybe now she can start living her life again. She deserves someone to take care of her."

I am going to take care of her. I promise.

I can take no more. I never dreamed Blaire's life has been so hard. It's no wonder she'd gotten so angry with me when I moved her out of her apartment and into the new one. She'd felt like I had put her down.

God, I'm such a fucking piece of shit!

I hear Blaire laughing with a nurse in the hallway and so I make my excuse to leave.

"I really need to be going, Ms. Michaels."

"But Mr. Ryder, I wish you'd stay. My daughter, Blaire, will be here shortly."

"I'm sorry. Please send her my regards. Good day, Ms. Michaels," I say hurriedly, rushing out the door.

Turning the corner, I collide into her. Everything happens around me in slow motion. Her silky, long, ebony waves swipe across my face, hypnotizing me with the scent of her delicious cherry smelling shampoo. My hands catch the sides of her arms just before the soft drink in her hands crashes against my chest, soaking my suit and her shirt.

"Oh my goodness! I'm so very sorry!" she apologizes, concern shining in her eyes.

Fuck me! Those eyes of hers! I could never deny her anything staring into them. Unlike mine, hers are bright and clear. They are not hazed by the dark. Heartbreakingly, they do have a hint of sadness and worry in them. Something I will do my damnedest to erase.

Her touch is more than I can handle. Pushing her away, I storm off down the hallway to get away from her while I still can.

Blaire

Drenched in my drink, I head to the ladies room to try to dry myself. Yanking the towels out of the dispenser, I curse him loudly as I turn to chunk my busted cup into the trash bin against the wall.

"What an asshole!" I exclaim, trying to absorb some of the drink out of my shirt with the paper towels.

What the hell is his problem? Does the man not know how to say a simple, "excuse me" or "I'm sorry"?

Don't mistake it; I'm more than thankful for what his company is doing for my mom. But why does the man have to treat me like this? And better yet, why is that when I am near him, I feel so drawn to him. My body reacts to him in ways I've never experienced before. One look into those chocolate eyes of his and I am lost. He is like a magnet to my soul.

After standing in front of the hand dryer for a few minutes, I walk away with a dry but coke stained shirt. When I finally get back to my mom's room, she is asleep. Instead of hanging around, I decide to go for a walk. Maybe I'll head down to the local market and pick up another cheap shirt or something.

The day is bright and sunny. It does nothing for my foul mood. I want this day to match how I feel, dark and stormy. I can't figure out how my life has gotten so fucked up all because of two men. One, who I can't get out of my head, and the other, who is a complete stranger.

What girl in her right mind would sell her body to another man? What girl would allow someone to do the sick things he does to me? What girl would love it so much?

That girl is me.

The time has gotten away from me while I've sat here on this wooden bench. This little park is one of my favorites in the city. Joggers run past me on the track and children laugh from the nearby playground. I wish I could be that carefree again, that innocent. I don't think I ever had the opportunity to be. I have always had to worry about someone else.

My phone from Mr. R chirps beside me.

Mr. R: 2934 W. Baker Street, 15 minutes

Baker Street? That's right across from me. What the fuck? This stalking shit is seriously going to have to stop.

Grabbing my purse from beside me, I leave the park entrance and cross the street. Looking up at the buildings, I scan them for the correct address. When I finally reach it, I'm confused. There is a for sale sign on the front of the building with tall brown weeds growing up near the sidewalk. Pushing open the iron gate, I hesitantly approach the front door and peek inside. Knowing that he is expecting me to be at this address, I reach for the doorknob and discover that it is unlocked. Nervously, I walk inside the dark foyer and reach for the light switch. When I flip the switch, nothing happens but a click. Trying the one on the adjacent wall does me no good either.

"Hello?" I call as I walk more into the heavy darkness ahead. I hear nothing, but creaking wooden floors beneath my feet.

"Hello?" I repeat myself, still with no answer. Reaching for my phone, I swipe the screen to text him back. I'd been so preoccupied with my message that I hadn't notice the door behind me close. It locks. I am grabbed from behind. Energy swirls all around me, growing and building like a vicious cyclone. I inhale his spice scent and relax against his strong chest. Instantly, I am no longer afraid.

Chapter Twenty-Six

Jaxxon

I need to let her go.

I need her.

I'd tracked her phone using the GPS app on mine. I know she is still nearby.

When I left the hospital, I'd circled this block at least twenty times before I'd laid eyes on an old building for sale. Its darkness intrigues me and draws me in. When I approach the broken windows, I peer inside and an idea overtakes me. It isn't hard for me to reach through the broken glass of the door and enter.

I wait in the darkness. I love it here. My demon calls to be fed and I desperately need to feel her in my arms every bit as much as I need air to breathe. I'd only given her 15 minutes to get here. There is no way I can wait any longer than that. My cock stands at full mast waiting to impale her. This time with her will be anything but sweet.

"Hello?" I hear her voice call from the front entrance.

The demon inside of me smiles.

Again, I hear her call out into the darkness.

"Hello?" This time there is a bit of terror in the way she speaks.

I love it!

Waiting for her to come in my direction, I stand beside the

door. I see her shadow move closer. The heat from her body can be felt as she walks past me. I breathe her in and make my move.

Blaire

"Raven," he whispers in my ear. The way he says it makes me tremble with anticipation.

I turn to him in the darkness. I can't see anything at all. Reaching up towards his face, I slide my hand across his cheek, and then lift the other up to do the same. Tenderly, I trace across his forehead and eyes, trailing my fingertips down to his lips. His hot mouth sucks my finger inside, triggering my clit to begin pounding in my panties. A loud moan escapes my mouth, and he releases my finger, hissing through his teeth.

The demon is awake.

I catch him by surprise when I don't submit to him. And for the first time ever, I take his control away.

Jaxxon

I have it all planned out what I am going to do to her in the dark. The thrill of it has me high. When she jumps into my arms, something snaps. Wrapping her long legs around my waist, her pussy pulls my cock to it with a relentless magnetic force. Blaire's lips crash to mine and I stumble forward, gripping her ass underneath her skirt. With a hard thud, her body slams against the wall behind her, knocking the breath out of her panting chest. Pressing the full weight of my body against her, I pin her tightly to the wall. My hands find the strings to the sides of her underwear. With one violent jerk, she is free. With one hand, I shove my pants down, dropping my boxer briefs with it. I don't have to see if she is wet because she always is. Cupping her plump firm ass in my hands, I shove her down as I thrust up. Her hot tight folds grip me with dear life on entry.

I'm in fucking Heaven.

Over and over, I thrust up into her. Dropping my head onto her neck, I begin biting her skin.

Blaire's nails violently tear at the skin on my back, causing me to bite harder into her skin.

"Goddamn, baby!" I yell as she begins rocking her hips in perfect sync with me.

She feels so damn terrific.

"Please. Don't. Stop!" she utters, struggling to catch her breath.

"Say it, Raven! Tell me to fuck you harder. Tell me what you want."

"Fuck me harder. Please, Sir."

Her words unravel me. All my emotions, the rage, the confusion, the hunger… I impale it in her. There is no doubt in my mind that we are busting the sheetrock behind her. Her back will be covered in bruises tomorrow, I'm sure.

"Yes!" Her loud screams bounce through the open room.

Then just when I think I have gained back control of this, she takes it away once more.

"Slow. Please, Sir, I want you to go slow."

Blaire

Nothing has ever felt as good as him fucking me against this wall. His hard cock slamming into my insides will inevitably leave me walking funny for the next day or so. But right now, I don't care if I ever walk right again. I want him to fuck me. Never could I have imagined the sensations that are rippling through me right now. My orgasm finds me with vengeance, leaving me gasping and desperate for more. Beads of sweat drip off his face and into my mouth as his forehead presses to mine. His salty taste is delectable.

"Slower. Please, Sir, go slow," I ask.

Immediately his forehead lifts and his thrusting stops.

What is he doing?

His salty lips find mine; his teeth bite hard against them, drawing blood. My pussy throbs harder. Mr. R's hot tongue swipes across my mouth, taking the blood with it. And then he starts moving, giving me slow, tender strokes. I feel every single ridge of his long thick cock rake against my inner walls. The building down low begins. Holding on for dear life, I wrap my arms around his neck and tighten the muscles in my thighs.

Mr. R's pants grow louder. The smell of our arousal fills the darkness that surrounds us. His long, torturous thrusting teases my sweet spot and I know my release is near.

"Come with me, please," I beg him, placing my mouth over his. Our tongues slowly roll around one another, tasting the other's soul a bit more.

"AHH!" I scream and he presses my ass hard with his hands.

Following my release, he fills me up with his cum.

He releases his grip and steadies me as my feet touch the floor. My knees nearly give way, but his arms are there to hold me up.

He doesn't speak for a long time. All I can hear is the rustling of clothes and the familiar sound of a zipper.

Say something. Please.

His warm palm cups my cheek.

"What are you thinking? Tell me."

"I'm thinking I don't know your name. I don't know anything about you."

"My name is Sir. We are almost to the end of our agreement. There is nothing more to know."

"I don't want this to end."

There. I have told him. It is the truth.

Fuck this stupid contract.

Fuck this dark room.

I just want him to admit he cares about me.

“This is business, Raven. I am sorry if you can’t understand that.”

“This is more than fucking business, and you know it!”

He remains quiet for a few seconds and then lets out a loud sigh.

“Raven, we both got what we wanted. I’m sorry if you believed there was going to be more to this arrangement.” He walks across room and out the door.

I want to run after him into the sunlight to expose him.

But I don’t. I stay in the dark alone and cry.

Chapter Twenty-Seven

Day 13

Jaxxon

I come into work today with vengeance. I hate the world and I hate everyone in it. Everyone, but her, that is.

Blaire.

Since I left her yesterday afternoon, I haven't eaten, slept, or stopped thinking about her. Not even for one goddamn second. She made me lie about how I felt. Why can't she just prove me right? Love isn't real. Someone always gets hurt. I will eventually hurt her and I'll never allow that to happen. I'll kill anyone who ever tries to harm her, and that includes myself. I'd just as soon ram a knife into my own heart than know I caused her any more pain in her life.

Storming into my father's office, I catch him in mid thrust, Chloe's ass bent up in the air, my father's head thrown back. It is revolting to see. This is my example. All my life, this is who has shown me how to treat women. He is nothing but a fucking sorry excuse for a father.

Chloe looks back around at me and smiles. I could've had her multiple times in the past, but I have grown tired of my father's sloppy seconds. My father roars his release inside her and backs away. The smug satisfied smile on his face sickens me.

"Next time lock the fucking door, Chloe!" my father barks at her when he sees me standing there. He pulls his pants back up, adjusts his suit, and pats Chloe on the butt as she leaves.

"What do you want, Jaxxon?" he says, perturbed.

I have to get out of this town for a while. Far away from Blaire.

"The Holbrook account. I want to take it over."

"Kent can handle it. Besides that, it would require you to work out of the London office."

"Yes, I know that, but I would like more responsibility. I think I have proven myself capable of that already."

"Fine. I will speak to Kent about it this afternoon. However, I warn you, if you fuck around over there, I'm not bailing you out of trouble. Understand?"

What an asshole!

"Yeah, I got it."

Slamming the door behind me, I can feel the blood boiling inside. Stacy picks the wrong fucking time to follow me in my office, pointing her finger in my chest.

"If you think for one minute that I am going to let you fuck me over, you are mistaken."

"Get out, Stacy!"

"No! Not until you tell me what I did wrong?" she pleas.

GREAT! Just fucking great!

"You and I were nothing more than a quick fuck and you know it. I'm sorry if you can't understand, but I'm not interested anymore."

"Baby, don't do this," she says, throwing herself on me

Baby? What the fuck? She is straight up crazy!

"Stacy, get off me! I told you I am not interested!" I yell, furiously shoving her off me.

Her blue eyes turn murderous and then I feel the slap of her hand across my face.

I'm an asshole. I deserve that.

"You bastard!"

I let that one go. She's right. I am one.

"I hope your next whore is worth it!"

Anger overtakes me. I want to break her neck for saying that about Blaire.

Before she can assault me again, I grab hold of her raised hand, and drag her to my office door.

"SECURITY!" I yell and two men come running down the hall.

"Escort this woman out of this building and be sure to destroy her employee badge! She is to be permanently banned from the premises. Understood?"

"Yes, Sir, Mr. Ryder," the tall security guard answers while dragging a screaming Stacy down the hall.

"Jaxxon!" My father screams at me. "In my office! NOW!"

Following him back to his office, he slams the door behind him.

"What the hell was that all about?"

"I handled it Father."

"Handled it? Yes, I saw exactly how you handled it. I want to tell you that I just got off the phone with the London office and they have made the arrangements for you to fly out this weekend."

"Thank you," I reply and turn to leave.

"Jaxxon, I would advise you focus on your career while in London instead of fucking the women in the office. I'll admit Ms. Mathers was a bit of trouble here."

I cringe at the revelation that he'd fucked her too.

Without answering him, I leave.

Fucking hypocrite.

Returning to my office, I pour a glass of bourbon and collapse in my chair. This time next week, I will be sitting in my new London office, far away from this town, my father, and Blaire.

Blaire

"It looks like they are letting me break out of here on Friday, Sweetheart," my mom jokes from the wheelchair I'm pushing. She is doing so well today that I decided to take her for a walk out around the hall. It is so good to see her in such good spirits. I should be so happy at her getting ready to come home, but I can't stop thinking about Mr. R.

He hasn't called or messaged me all day and I don't know what to make of it. Maybe he's already replaced me with someone else. Maybe I had been wrong and he didn't care for me at all. How stupid does this make me?

We finally return to her room and I help her settle back in the bed.

"You look so tired, Blaire. Why don't you go home and lay down?"

"I'm fine, Mom." I reply while pulling the covers over her.

"Tell me what is bothering you, please, Baby."

"Really, I'm good," I say. Maybe it is better I go home. I'm not good company anyways.

"I think I'm going to head home, I'm feeling more tired than I thought."

She grabs my hand and squeezes.

"I love you so much, Sweetheart. Things are going to get better for us now. I promise."

Somehow, for me, I don't think things will ever be better.

Jaxxon

I don't call her.

I can't.

Every part of my body needs her. She is the fire in my soul. Because of her, my demon sleeps. Don't think it hasn't crossed my mind just to march two floors down and show her what she has done to me. I want to take her into my arms and tell her something that I desperately need her to know.

I love her.

Yes, I love her.

Do I want to let go of her tomorrow?

Of course not! But I need to.

The night air blows across my face as I stand on my rooftop deck. The city is still alive below me, but that is hard for me to believe when I feel so dead inside. The papers on the table outside begin to rustle, reminding me of where I'd laid them.

The contract.

This stupid fucking packet of nonsense has done nothing but bring me grief and suffering. I had been an arrogant and selfish asshole to insist she do this. Caring for her was never supposed to happen. I don't know how to care, how to love. When I think of what I've done and what I've taken from her, it isn't any wonder where my soul is destined.

Straight to hell.

She's sacrificed everything for her mother. Blaire has shown me a kind of love that I never thought existed.

Unconditional, beautiful love.

It isn't a fairy tale; it isn't extinct. It lives through her. It now lives through me. Coursing through these once icy, cold-blooded bastard's veins is love. She's transformed me.

She is the antidote to my poisoned soul.

I have to fix this. I can't do this to her another second. Even though this is the thirteenth day, it's over.

All of it is over.

Blaire

When I wake up this morning, my heart hurts. I am so empty inside without him. Patting the covers next to me, I search for my phone. I had slept with it in my arms in hopes he would call. The call that, of course, never happened.

As I pad my way out into the brightly lit apartment, I shield my eyes from the sun. I know now what a vampire must feel because I quickly search for a dimmer spot in the kitchen to hide.

After I've finished my cup of coffee, I sense my body finally awakening. Pouring another cup, I grab a granola bar and a banana, and then head to the living room. Just as I am about to sit my cup down, a black envelope on my table catches my eyes.

My name is beautifully written on the gray tab on the front. There is no doubt whom it's from or how it had gotten there. He'd come in here last night and left it. For the life of me, I can't understand why he didn't wake me.

Picking up the envelope, I allow it to rest in my lap. It feels so heavy against my legs. My mind races as to what it could be. With only one way to put the torture out of my system, I lift the flap and tear it open. Holding my breath, I close my eyes and reach in to retrieve whatever is inside. When I finally get the courage to open my eyes, my heart drops. My hands are trembling so much that I drop the contents on the floor. There on the hardwood floor lies my contract ripped in half, and now thanks to him, I officially have the heart that matches it.

Like a zombie for the rest of the day, I go through the motions of my monotonous life. Everything inside of me is numb and uncaring. Standing before my bathroom mirror, I see a ruined, dirty girl, a whore, someone who no one will ever want.

Chapter Twenty-Nine

Day 14

Blaire

Late into the night, I am awakened.

The darkness that lives inside of him calls me. I can feel it commanding me.

Wrapping my black, short silk robe around me, I prepare to go to him.

In a daze, I wander onto the elevator and slide in my key. Moments later, it stops at Level 9 and the doors open. I hesitate, unsure of whether or not I am losing my mind, or if this is actually real.

Bravely, I step off and continue walking ahead. I can't explain it, but the room in the far back pulls me to it. Like a moth to a flame, I enter.

The two long walls of tall windows saturate the room in rich glowing moonlight. A massive, king-sized canopy bed sits on a raised platform in the middle of the room. Adorned in white, luxurious linens and pillows, the bed makes the room look so peaceful and inviting. To be on this floor, this whole scene seems out of place. Shouldn't there be shackles and swings everywhere? This looks too normal, too intimate.

Dragging my hand across the soft white bedding, I continue to gravitate towards the windows. When I stare down at the traffic below, I spot a woman getting out of a cab. I wonder what her life is like. Is she is happy? Then I see a man come up and pull her into his arms. Of course, she is happy. She has someone who loves her. Her life is not sick and fucked up like mine.

Turning around, I sadly walk back to the large bed and crawl up onto it. It feels like heaven, lying back against the soft fabric. Catching a glimpse of the mirrored canopy above me, I stare at the person looking back at me.

Who is this girl?

If I had something I could throw and break the mirror with, I would.

Reaching in the pocket of my robe, I pull out my blindfold, secure it around my face, and fall back to the bed.

He is close. I can feel him.

Jaxxon

He has finally awakened in me. I should have known that he wouldn't stay quiet for long. A day is too long without the feel of her body, without her love. My demon and I are both in agony. I want to give up and walk away from her, but the darkness that resides deep inside won't let me.

Shuffling out of bed, I go to where I am summoned. Maybe when the demon sees that the space is empty, it will die. Then I can finally be at peace.

The floor is dark and quiet. From the moment I step off the elevator, I am pulled. When I find myself standing at the last door on the far side of the room, I lean my head against the door and close my eyes.

The room.

Damn this fucking room!

I had done it all for her. She deserves a place that isn't about torture and pain. I had wanted some way to show her peace in what we share together and to prove that there is light even in the dark. I need her to see that she is my light.

The demon laughs at me, relentlessly mocking me. Angrily, I proceed to push open the door, preparing to destroy every inch of the room.

Heaven has found Hell and it's now laying in my bed, fast asleep.

Blaire.

My perfect magnificent angel glows in the moonlight, looking so peaceful as she sleeps. Her long ebony waves cascade around her shoulders, draping over her flawless olive skin. Her short, black silk robe teases me by being slightly open, exposing her black panties, and showing off her long sexy as fuck legs. I'm so transfixed by her that I don't realize I've been standing here holding my breath. Quietly, I inch closer.

As I approach the bed, I see the blindfold and my heart pulls. My beautiful submissive angel has come to me.

Gently, I place a knee on the bed and lean over to kiss her. The moment my lips taste hers, I am lost. Her mouth opens to my urgency, giving me exactly what I crave. I've missed her so goddamn much and it's only been one fucking day. Sliding my arm underneath her back, I pull her in closer. Her soft hands run through my hair, tugging fiercely as our hunger grows deeper. I never stop kissing her as I tug on the sash of her robe, yanking it open. Leaning up, I run my hand down her chest, proceeding down to her toned stomach. Her beautiful body arches at my touch as her legs fall open.

Sweet Jesus, that is a gorgeous sight. My dick is so fucking hard for her.

Moving my lips to her stomach, I throw her legs over my shoulders and shove my nose into her core. The black lace is soaked with her juices and her scent intoxicates me. Her delicious smell is like the rarest aphrodisiac. I want it all to myself. I will kill anyone who ever touches her. She is mine.

Yanking down her panties, I watch her lift her ass for me to take them off. Kissing up her inner thigh, I dig my fingernails into the back of her legs while pulling her drenched pussy to my mouth. Plunging my tongue inside of her, I suck every drop of her down. I'm insatiable when it comes to her.

"Please! Don't stop! Yes! OH GOD! YES!" she screams, arching her back and gripping the sheets above her. With my other hand, I yank down my boxers and ram inside of her.

FUCK!

I have never been this hard.

Over and over, I impale her with my hot, throbbing cock. I grab her hands and slam them above her head, pinning her down as I pound into her sweet pussy.

"You feel so goddamn good, Baby," I growl, shoving myself deep into her. The canopy bed shakes so violently that I'm sure we are going to break it.

"Come for me!" I order.

Her pussy instantly clamps down on me, and I feel her body climb to her release. I fight hard to not come in her.

"That's it, Baby, come on my dick!"

"Please, Sir. Take me harder! Yes!" she screams.

I flip her onto her knees and pull her back against me, slapping her ass. Lining up to her opening, I enter her hard and quick from behind. She yelps and then lets out a loud moan, driving more into the demon's madness.

"Give me more of that ass!" I demand and she pushes back against me.

Forcefully, I tug her hair, making her sit upright to take me.

"Fuck that dick, Baby! Yeah!" I snarl. My demon roars in delight.

Slap! Slap! I smack her ass harder. Her skin is glowing red.

"Spank me harder, Sir," she begs and the demon inside of me fills with pride. She has no idea what she is doing to me.

Grabbing her hair again, I pull out of her and turn her to face me. Taking both my hands, I push her head down, forcing her to take my dick into her mouth.

"Suck me clean! Taste your cum!" I order, hissing loudly when her lips seal tightly around my cock.

Fuck yes!

"See how fucking delicious you are?"

"Mmmm," she moans and I shove her head harder up and down. I fight the urge to come in her mouth, but she is driving me insanely close to my release. I let her go and bring her hips upward, positioning her over me. Propped up on the pillows behind mc, I sit up while she rides me.

"Ride me! Slam that pussy down on my cock!" I command. I watch her glorious full tits bounce up and down above me. Her long waves cascade down her back. I cup her ass into my hands and thrust upward in her, matching her rhythm.

"Oh… my God, YES!" She explodes all over my dick. Her nails dig deep into my chest, drawing streaks of blood.

Spiraling to my own release, I grab her waist, holding it down as I drench her insides with my cum. I can't hold it back. Her name erupts through my lips in a scream.

"Blaire!" I shout as my vision goes blurry from my orgasm.

When I blink again, it clears, but my euphoria leaves when she reaches up and unties the blindfold from her face.

Oh, God, No!

With my throbbing cock still inside of her, my angel looks down upon her demon. Her dark eyes are confused and full of hurt. My chest constricts with pain.

"No!" she gasps, jumping off me. With eyes pained, she scampers off the bed, shielding herself with her hands.

"Let me explain." I beg, leaping off the bed to go to her. I tenderly touch her arm, but she jerks away, looking at me with broken expression.

"Get your motherfucking hands off me! How could you?" she screams with tears in her beautiful dark eyes.

I just want to hold her in my arms; I want to kiss away those tears. I want to make this right, but no matter what I do, I can't. The damage has been done.

"Has it been you all along?" she asks through her cries. I shamefully nod in response, watching her shoulders slump in sadness.

NO! I can't lose her!

"Why? Why would you do this to me?" Her voice shakes with despair.

There is no right answer to give. I don't know what to say.

"I'm sorry, Blaire," I apologize, while handing her black robe to her.

She furiously jerks it out of my hands.

Her fury feeds the evil. The demon inside me loves seeing this, but it's killing me to watch her come apart.

"Sure, you're sorry! This has all been a funny game for you, hasn't it? I'm sure it was some elaborate plan for you to get your sick fucking thrills off having some desperate virgin. You have NO idea what you have done! I gave up everything for this. Everything!"

"I know! GOD! I KNOW!" I scream, while yanking at my hair. "Do you think for one goddamn minute that this has been easy for me? You were never supposed to tell me no that night at the club in the first place! I had to have you! You gave me no choice."

"Had to have me, huh? Is that why you made me sign that goddamn contract and blackmailed me with those pictures? All because you had to have me?"

"Yes, it was, but the contract wasn't real. I made it all up, Blaire. I had to. One night with you would never have been enough for me. Fuck! Even a thousand nights with you would never be enough."

"FUCK YOU!" she screams.

"Blaire, you have to listen to me!"

"I don't have to listen to a damn thing! You used me." She spits angrily at me before continuing. "You had me from the first time I saw you in that club. I have never wanted anything more in my life. But none of that mattered to you then, because you wasted no time shoving your dick in Honey's mouth."

"STOP!" I shout at her, but she doesn't.

The truth hurts. She's wanted me from the beginning just as much as I've wanted her, but then I went and fucked all of that up!

"I was wrong to have done that, but I got so angry when you turned me down. The whole time I was with her, I was thinking of you. You have to believe me! When you found us, I stopped Honey and ran after you. Don't you remember me coming out into the parking lot that night?"

"Jesus! Give me a fucking break! Really? You expect me to believe that? Is that why you brought her back here and paid her to do all of those things to me while I was strapped to a chair? What did you expect? A happy, willing threesome?"

"No, Goddamnit! I wanted to push you beyond your limits and get you to submit to me. Every time I'm with you, I lose more of myself. I wanted you to be reminded of who's in control. When I chose Honey, I thought it would be easier on you to do those things with a girl that you know. I didn't think."

"Easier? EASIER? Who gives a fuck about making ANYTHING easier on me? You say you were the one who didn't have a choice, but that's not true! I'm the one that didn't have the choice! I couldn't let my mom die! I did the only thing I could do to get that kind of money. I gave you everything I had, and now I have nothing." She laughs wildly. It scares the living shit out of me. Her eyes are glassy; her heart is breaking. All of this is torturing her to have to relive this in her mind.

Without warning, Blaire storms out and darts across the hall to the worst room on this floor. My mind is spinning, but I remain right on her heels. Grabbing the nearby crop off the wall, she turns, and unexpectedly delivers a hard blow across my bare chest. Over and over, she hits me in the same spot. With each thrashing, she grows more and more exhausted. I could have stopped her, but I allow her to continue. I deserve it. I need to feel this pain; her pain is mine to own.

Fourteen lashes.

"One for each fucking day of your precious, damn contract."

Broken and breathless, she snaps the crop in half and drops it to the floor. My skin is in agony, but I could care less. I deserve everything she unleashes at me.

"I want you to know that you are the only person I've ever wanted," I plead.

"Well, guess what? I wanted you! That's right! The whole time Mr. R was fucking me, I was imagining it to be you. Now, I wish I'd never taken that damn blindfold off! I wish I never laid eyes on you! You've ruined me! I'm sick and disgusting! You've turned me into a whore, and worst of all, I let you! No one will ever want me now!" She cries hysterically, bolting from the room.

"Blaire! Stop!" I demand, but she doesn't.

I reach the elevator door just as it's closing. I take my hand and force it back open. She slaps it away.

"Don't touch me! Your fourteen days are up! This is all just business, remember?"

And with that, the doors to the elevator shut and the love of my life leaves me to rot in my own hell.

Chapter Thirty

Blaire

I can't breathe.

God, it hurts so bad! Please make it stop!

Jolting up from the bed, I see that it is already morning. I'm so nauseous that I don't want to chance putting anything on my stomach. I want to forget him. God knows I need to.

When I go to dress, I absentmindedly pull out a skirt and then I chunk it across the closet. Yanking down a pair of jeans, I slip them on and pull a shirt over my head. Not wanting to mess with makeup or my hair, I shove a baseball cap on my head and put on a pair of sunglasses to hide my puffy eyes.

My mom is beaming when I walk into the room.

"Oh, Sweetheart! Good, you're here! The doctor just gave me the okay for an early discharge. Isn't that wonderful?" she exclaims excitedly.

"That's wonderful, Mom." I force a smile.

"Baby girl, what's the matter? You still look so tired, Blaire."

"I'm fine, Mom! I've just been so busy getting our new place ready," I lie.

"Well, now that I am feeling better, I'm going to make sure you rest! No more taking care of me."

Thankfully, we are interrupted by a nurse walking into her room.

“Hi, Ms. Michaels. I’m just here to take your vitals so we can begin the discharge process.”

“Mom, I’m going to go downstairs and grab a quick bite. I’ll be right back.”

“Sure, Sweetheart,” she replies and I shut the door behind me.

Food is the last thing on my mind, but Jaxxon isn’t. Since I last saw him, I’ve been miserable. I can’t eat and I can’t sleep. I look like hell and I feel even worse. I wish I could say there is a cure for this, but there isn’t.

Jaxxon Ryder is my incurable disease.

A couple of hours later, my mom is officially released from the hospital. I call a cab for us and wait by her wheelchair with her for it to arrive. To my surprise, Parker pulls up to entrance in the familiar black Range Rover to pick us up. I just pray he uses discretion and doesn’t saying anything in front of my mom.

“Hello, Ms. Michaels. Mr. Ryder wanted to ensure you arrived home comfortably,” he says before taking her arm and helping her into the SUV. I don’t even bother looking in him the eye as I step in and slide beside my mom in the back seat.

“Mr. Ryder is such a wonderful man. He’s given us a new chance at life. I will forever be indebted to what his company has done for us.”

No, you won’t! I’ve already paid that debt in full with my soul.

I try to swallow the sorrow in the back of my throat. I don’t want her to see me upset because then I won’t be able to hold anything back.

When we pull up to the apartment building, my nerves overtake me. How am I supposed to explain all of this to my mom?

“Good afternoon, James,” I smile at the sweet doorman. His eyes twinkle and then his face lights up when he sees my mom.

Even just out of the hospital, she looks stunning.

“Good afternoon, Blaire and to you, too, Ms. Michaels.”

My mom smiles at him and takes his hand. James helps lead her through the lobby while Parker brings our things inside. I become surprised when both of them follow us up to the apartment. Parker sets her things inside the door and James sweetly helps my mom to the couch.

Parker hesitates when I follow him to the door to let him out.

“Thank you for picking us up. Please tell Mr. Ryder we appreciate his kindness.”

“Ms. Blaire, please talk to him. I’ve never seen him like this before. I’ve worked for him for seven years now, and not once has he ever been this way over anyone.”

Opening the door, I try to contain the pain inside me. I want nothing more than to go to him, but he has destroyed me.

“I can’t,” I whisper and dare a glance up at Parker’s concerned eyes.

“Good day, Ms. Blaire. Call me if you need anything,” he says, handing me a card.

When I return to the living room, James is laying a blanket over my mom. It’s more than obvious that he is smitten with her.

“Blaire, James was just telling me that he lives in this building, too.”

I smile knowingly at her.

“Well, I really must be getting back downstairs. It is nice to finally meet you, Ms. Michaels.”

“Please, call me Madison,” my mom replies sweetly. The flirting between the two of them is unreal.

Embarrassed, he blushes and nods at me.

“If there is anything you need, I am only a call away.”

“Thank you, James,” I reply and he lets himself out of the apartment. Walking back into the living room, I can’t help but notice my mom's face beaming with happiness.

"Blaire, this place is wonderful! But how on Earth are we able to afford this?"

I come up with an explanation where I don't have to lie, but I don't tell her the entire truth either. I never will.

"Our old apartment building was bought by someone who was wanting to renovate it. Mr. Ryder learned of the situation and insisted we stay here for the time being."

"My goodness! Our luck just keeps getting better and better."

"Do you have to go into work tonight?"

I hesitate again before altering the truth once more.

"No, my work has given me time off to take care of you."

"Well, that is going to end right now. First things first, I insist you go take a long hot bath and lie down. I don't want you fretting over me a minute more! I'm feeling better every day."

"Mom."

"Yes, that is right. I am your mom. Now, go do as I say," she says sternly, but with a smile.

After getting her settled, I decide to humor her and do as she says. Maybe when I wake up, I will feel better.

Panting loudly, my eyes jolt open. My hand is between my legs, nestled deep into my panties, which are soaked from my dream. Even in my sleep, I can't escape him. He invades every part of my being.

How am I ever going to survive him?

Stretching, I get out of bed. It takes me a moment or two before I am able to steady myself. I feel worse now than I did before I laid down. I guess I must have slept too long.

Stepping out into the living room, I see that it is already almost evening time. My mom is curled on the couch asleep. Quietly, I inch closer and pull the covers up a bit on her. While she is resting, I need to get out of this building and get some air.

Although I'm not exactly sure how, I have to get my head clear and I can't do that here.

All the way down to the elevator lobby, I stare at the number 9 on the elevator panel. It taunts me, beckoning me to return to it. I notice the key slot above the 9 and can't help but wonder what is on the top level. When the door opens, the conversation at the lobby desk echoes in the foyer.

"James, this is Mr. Ryder's extra key to the penthouse."

Penthouse? He lives here? Of course he lives here! God, I am so fucking stupid! That is why he wanted me to live here.

Marcus hands James a silver chain with a key on it. It looks just like the one I have.

"Yes, Sir. What time will the new girl be here to pick it up?"

New girl?

"Mr. Ryder says she will be here sometime tomorrow."

"Yes, Sir. I will make sure to give her the key."

He'd told me that he loves me. Now he has already moved on with someone else!

I hate him!

I love him.

My empty stomach twists and turns. Covering my mouth, I make a dash for the bathroom next to me. James notices me as I run past him to throw up. Lifting the lid, I barely make it in time before hurling into the toilet. Because I haven't eaten anything, nothing but bile comes up with each heave.

Make it stop. Please make this hurt inside go away.

Running cold water into the sink, I cup a handful and take a small drink before splashing my flushed face. Everything around me is spinning a bit, but I think if I can just get some air, things will be better.

"Blaire? Are you alright?" James meets me at the door when I exit the bathroom.

"Yes, I'm fine. Just something I ate."

"Why don't you let me help you back upstairs? You look awfully pale."

"I'm fine, James," I say, blinking away the dizzy spell.

"I'm going to go for a walk. I just need some fresh air."

"Blaire, I don't think-," I interrupt him.

"I'll be fine!" I snap and turn to walk out the door. The phone rings, and I hear James answer it as I leave.

The sunshine and fresh air don't seem to be helping me. Convincing myself that I just need to get a little farther away from the building, I continue walking. My feet carry me ahead unknowingly while my mind goes somewhere far from here.

So much of me wants to believe him, to understand him, but the rest of me knows he is poisoning me. A strong aroma of Italian food hits me, and I blink out of the daze I've been walking in. I know I have to turn around and head back. I can't call a cab or anyone because I left my phone and wallet at home.

My body feels so weak. My stomach still twists inside with reminders of earlier.

Another woman. He's replaced me.

Nausea hits me again, this time worse than before. Even though there is nothing left to come up, my stomach still keeps heaving. Quickly, I dart to the alley and brace my hand against the brick wall. I blink, but the world is getting so dark and black. I try to walk forward to find someone to help me, but my body is not letting me move. A tall figure is just ahead. If only I can make it to them. Each step is harder and harder. My pulse pounds in my ears, my knees give way.

I'm falling, but someone catches me.

"Blaire!" he screams. I'm so out of it that I don't know if he is real or a dream. I reach up, but then I give into the darkness.

Jaxxon

I stare up at her window from the back seat of the Range Rover. Regret fills me inside at what I'd done. Some things we do just have no rhyme or reason to them. But she is my rhyme; she is my reason. I'm scheduled to leave tonight for London. My bags are already loaded in the back, and boxes in my place will be shipped to my new place tomorrow. Perhaps if I can put distance between us, we can both heal. Who am I kidding? I'll never be the same.

Parker just dropped off my extra key to Marcus for my new housekeeper to clean the place and cover the furniture. I don't know when I will be back in the States, but I will definitely have to move out of this building now. I can no longer live that close to her and not have her.

Parker emerges and settles behind the steering wheel.

"Ready, Sir?" he asks, looking at me in the rearview mirror.

"Yes," I answer hesitantly and then he pulls away from the curb.

Traffic is so backed up after only a block, leaving everyone at a complete standstill. Digging out my phone, I get a chill down my back. Turning my head, I see long black waves bounce against her back.

Blaire.

Expressionless, she stares out ahead. It's almost as if her body is on autopilot of some sort.

Where is she going this late in the evening?

Traffic still isn't moving. When she begins disappearing out of my sight, fear and desperation overtake me. Opening the back SUV door, I run down the sidewalk to catch up to her, still staying back enough she doesn't see me following. Twelve long blocks later, she suddenly stops and turns in my direction. I quickly hide, shielding myself behind a large restaurant sign. Carefully, I dare a peek around to find her studying her surroundings. The confused look on her face indicates she isn't sure where she is or how she got there.

Unexpectedly, she takes off running towards the little alley beside of the restaurant. Panicked, I follow in pursuit. I find her facing away from me, bracing against the wall, throwing up. When she turns back around, I can see she isn't well. No longer caring if she is pissed at me or not, I head towards her. She walks her hands across the wall for support and then her knees give way. I am there to catch her just as she falls.

"Blaire!" I shout, and for a moment, I think she is going to touch my face.

Scooping her in my arms, I carry her towards the sidewalk where Parker has parked and is running to open the back door.

She mumbles something, then blinks awake.

"Blaire. Are you all right?"

"What happened?" she asks weakly.

"You passed out. I'm taking you to the hospital."

"No, please don't. My mom will be worried. Really! I'm fine now."

"Damn it, Blaire!"

"Just take me home."

Hesitating, I ask Parker to return us back to the building.

When we arrive, James meets us with a concerned look on his face. Lifting her back up off the ground, I don't allow her to walk. Cradling her in my arms, I walk towards where he is standing.

"Ms. Blaire. Are you alright?"

"She's fine, James. Do me a favor. Call Dr. Martin and ask him to come up to my apartment. Don't alarm Ms. Michaels. If she calls, just explain that Blaire is with me."

"Yes, Sir." he answers while picking the phone up to call the doctor.

I walk Blaire to the elevator and slide my key into the penthouse level.

"Where are we going?" She blinks again in confusion.

“My place.”

“Just let me go back to my apartment, Jaxxon.”

“You are not well. I’ve called the doctor to come up and take a look at you.”

“Put me down!” she orders, slapping my arm, but I ignore her.

When we arrive, I carry Blaire into the living room and lay her on the couch. Weakly, she settles back against it, scanning the room. She eyes the boxes on the far wall and then turns to me with a questioning look on her face.

“What are all of those for?” she asks, pointing at the cardboard boxes.

“I’m moving to London.”

“What?” she asks, wild-eyed and breathless.

“I’m heading a new account over there for my family’s company.”

“When did you decide this?” she asks.

“The day I tore up the contract.”

“When do you leave?” The panic grows more evident in her questions.

“Tonight. I was on my way to the airport when I saw you.”

The doorbell rings and I move to answer it. Dr. Martin is a retired doctor that lives on the fourth floor.

“Hello Jaxxon, James said you needed me to come up.”

Leading him to Blaire, I explain what has happened and he asks for privacy while he examines her. I won’t say how much that fucking pisses me off. I know her own body better than she does.

After what seems like a year, he is finally through with her. He is placing a blanket over her sleeping body just as I walk in.

“Is she going to be all right?” I whisper, trying to not wake her.

He motions for me to follow him, concern evident on his face.

"Son, she is exhausted and extremely dehydrated. I made her drink something for me, but she still needs lots of fluids and plenty of rest. I gave her something to help her sleep. She'll be fine in a couple of days."

I can put London off for a bit. I can't leave her like this.

"Thank you, Sir. How much do I owe you?"

"You don't owe me a dime boy, you know that! Tell you what, how about you and I hit the course next time you're back in town?"

"That sounds like a plan," I reply, smiling.

Once I see him out, I return to her.

I'd instructed James to phone her mother and briefly explain what had happened. She, of course, became terrified and insisted that he bring her up to my place to ensure Blaire was all right. We decided it to be best that she stay the night, so I settled Ms. Michaels into the guest room and put Blaire in my bed.

My bed.

Standing over her, I take in the sight of her lying on my bed, allowing the memory to be permanently etched into my brain.

She belongs here.

Gently, I sit on the bed beside her and brush away a loose curl from her face. She smiles in her sleep and then resumes in peaceful slumber. The need I have for her is so intense that I can't help it. I have to be near her. She is the only fucking thing in my life that matters. Crawling in behind her, I pull her in close to me. She settles back against me, still not wakening. I breathe in her cherry shampoo and, for the first time in my life, I feel complete and whole. Here, in my arms, lies everything I will ever want and need, everything I can never have.

My eyes grow heavy, but I don't want to let go of her. Instead, I hold on a little longer, afraid of the feelings that will return if I don't. When the morning light hits me, I awaken to her dark eyes staring down at me.

Goddamn, she is fucking beautiful.

"How are you feeling?" I ask her, sitting up.

"I'm better. Thank you."

Pushing myself on up, I quickly get out of bed.

"Are you hungry?"

"No." Her answer is cold and quick. If she wants to play this game, she will never win.

"Well, you're going to eat. What would you like? I'll have it delivered?" I ask, stretching as I walk to the kitchen. Looking around, I don't see her mom anywhere.

"Where is your mom? I'll order something for all of us."

"I already had James help her back to our apartment."

"Oh, well, then you should be laying down."

"I'm fine," she barks at me. Anger rages in her eyes.

"Drink then!" I say, shoving a bottle of juice into her face.

"Do it now, Blaire! The doctor said if you didn't, you'd get worse."

She complies, but not happily. I don't care as long as she fucking drinks the damn thing.

"Dr. Martin has already been up to check on me. He says I'm fine. I just needed to catch up on sleep."

"Blaire, I–"

She interrupts me.

"I just wanted to say thank you. I don't want to stick around for your new girl."

"My new girl? What are you talking about?"

"Don't play stupid, Jaxxon. I know, all right? I overheard Marcus talking with James yesterday. They said a new girl was coming up today."

I don't even have time to respond when the front door opens

unexpectedly. Blaire's gorgeous face drops when she sees her. The moment I turn my head, I know I am fucked.

Chapter Thirty-One

Blaire

A blonde goddess stands before me in a short tight black uniform. She looks every bit as shocked to see me, as I am to see her.

“Oh, I’m sorry. I didn’t mean to interrupt. The doorman gave me the key, Mr. Ryder.”

“Your services are no longer needed. I’ll make sure you get paid for the job. Please, just leave us,” he says coldly, without taking his eyes from mine. The beautiful woman nods and leaves the apartment.

“Mr. Ryder, huh? So she gets to call you by your real name. Nice!” I spit angrily at him and storm out of the room, heading for the door.

“BLAIRE! Wait!” he yells, but I keep moving. Suddenly, his hand grips around my arm and spins me around to face him.

“She’s my new housekeeper! My old one is dealing with family health problems. I asked the agency to send me someone to clean the place after I left.”

“Well, enjoy that little fantasy then! Just maybe, if you call her right now, her ‘services’ will still be available.”

“Goddamn it, Blaire! I love you! Why can’t you see that?” He charges in front of me, blocking me from leaving. I can see the hurt and the pain in his eyes. It is real. His wounds are deep and raw.

I can't help it. I know I shouldn't, but I love him!

"How can you stand there and say that you love me? You obviously don't even know what love is!" I shout at him, hitting him in the chest.

He grabs my hands and pulls me closer to him. His touch makes me melt. His smell calms me.

"You're right. I didn't know what it was, not until you."

"Don't," I beg, no longer able to hold in my tears.

Taking a deep breath, he continues his confession.

"All my life, I've watched my father bring his whores in and out of our house. My mother didn't even give a damn. She'd just leave me to go on another vacation with one of her many boy toys while my father showed me a different love, the kind with belts and fists. I have never mattered to him. I've never mattered to anyone except my Grandfather, and he's gone now."

"If you hate your father so much, then why do you choose to be like him?"

"Because there is a part of me inside that won't let me free. A part of me will always need to stay in control. When I feel it slipping away, it calls me back into the dark."

"But Jaxxon, taking power is not love. Giving power is what love is about. I would have freely given what you've forced others to give you."

"Why?" he asks, looking at me desperately.

Taking his face in my hands, I look directly in his chocolate brown eyes. I can see now why he is so tortured. When I look at him, I see the sad little boy staring back at me. He only wants to be loved and accepted. Despite everything, I love this man with all of my heart. He needs to know this. He needs to hear this.

"Because I love you, Jaxxon Ryder. That's why."

His eyes close to my words. When he reopens them, they are full of tears.

"You can't love me, Blaire. Look at what I've done to you. I won't ever be able to forgive myself for that."

"Everything you've done, I've allowed. No matter the reasons, I am the one who chose this. You and I share something unexplainable. This between us has always been more than about some stupid contract."

"You deserve someone who doesn't need to dominate you. You deserve to be in control of your own life."

"Jaxxon, most of my life I've always had to be in control, even when I didn't want to be. I've met that demon inside you, and it doesn't scare me. It makes me forget every worry, every trouble in my life. It shows me pleasure from my own pain. Don't you see? I need that part of you just as much as I need you."

"I'm too lost in the darkness to be found," he says, defeated.

"Then let me be your light. When you get lost, I will show you the way home. I need you. I love you so much, Jaxxon."

Jaxxon

My angel.

Dropping to my knees, shame oozes from my pours. Shielding my face with my hands, I feel the regret pour over me. As much as I need her, I don't deserve her. I feel her kneel beside me. Her sweet soft hands pull both of mine away from my face. Leaning in, she squeezes my hands, causing me to look back into those beautiful eyes.

"I forgive you," she whispers against my lips. "Now, forgive yourself."

I submit fully to her. My demon raises the white flag.

I surrender.

"I love you, Baby. I'll do anything. Hit me, beat me, anything you want! Just please, PLEASE, don't leave me," I beg, grabbing onto her for dear life.

“I’m here, Jaxxon. I’m not going anywhere,” she whispers in my ear and I smile against her skin. Relief fills my body, but so does my hunger for her.

“Oh, yes you are,” I reply, kissing her neck. “You’re going back to my bed.” Crashing my lips to hers, we stand back up off the floor. Playfully, I lift her up and she wraps her long legs around my waist. Her dark waves fall around my face as I walk us back to my room. Holding our intense stare, we slowly begin removing each other’s clothes, allowing our hands to freely roam each other’s body.

Leaning forward, I urge her body to fall back against the bed. Moving between her legs, I can feel the heat radiating from her wet folds.

“You are so beautiful,” I say, leaning in and kissing her gently on the lips. Her dark eyes bashfully look away, but I pull her chin up, making her look back up at me.

“Never look away, Blaire. I need to always see your eyes. They are the light that guides me out of the dark.”

Then, as I slowly ease into her, I watch my demon submit to my angel, my light over the dark.

EPILOGUE

It's been ten months since I took off that blindfold. Ten months of complete and utter happiness. Ten months of finally knowing what it feels like to live. Looking back now, I can't believe I had not realized it had been him all along. The obvious signs were all around me, yet I'd seemed to stay blind to them all.

I'm sure you are wondering if we use the blindfold anymore. The answer is no. We no longer need it. Neither of us wants to hide from each other. I want to see his love for me; I crave that intense connection with him.

I think there had been lots of reasons he'd used it in the first place. At first, he had said it was to protect his identity, but I think with me, it had been far more than that. He'd meant to protect me from seeing what lived so deep within him.

Somehow, my beautiful man believed that if I ever saw it, I would run. He had feared his own reflection in my eyes, because he knew it mocked him. He knows now that I need them both. I am not afraid of either of them, no matter how dark he gets. Together they make him who he is, the man I will love for eternity.

My mom is doing magnificently. Nowadays, I can't seem to make her slow down any at all! Her radiant spirit inspires me every day. She and James are dating, and I've never seen her more happy. Thankfully, she still lives in the same apartment that Jaxxon moved us into. Because of that, I get to see her almost every day. I love having her so close to us because it makes me feel safe having everyone I love near me.

After we had made up, Jaxxon had wasted no time asking me to move in with him. Actually, if I am to be more accurate, he had insisted on it. But despite his demands, there is no way I would want it any differently. He owns my soul and I can't be without him. I need him beside me every night, forever. We belong together. We always have and we always will.

My mom hadn't been as shocked as I thought she'd be when I told her about Jaxxon and I being in love. Instead of the lecture I'd expected, she'd told me how happy she was to see me with someone who loved me so much. In the beginning, she'd seen the way we looked at each other and knew there was more to the story. I've never told my mom about how Jaxxon and I met. That story is only ours to know. It's a part of my life I treasure, and a part I'd rather forget. At any cost, to have what I have now, I'd do it all over again in a heartbeat.

Through the encouragement of him and my mom, I finished the few classes I needed to finish my degree. I'd never seen Jaxxon more proud than when I walked across that stage to get my diploma. With both of them cheering me on, along with some of my friends from school, I had never felt so loved.

Thankfully, Jaxxon turned down the account in London to stay here with me. Since my mom had been such a successful case, Jaxxon insisted that I come to work for him to help with PR for Ryder Technology. At first, I thought working together wouldn't be a very good idea. I certainly don't care for his father, nor the way he treated Jaxxon. But when I came to realize that I could promote a wonderful company and be in the arms of the man I love anytime I wanted, well, it became a no brainer to say yes. We get LOTS of work done in those private office meetings, let me tell you! Just not the work we need to be doing when we have an important project coming up.

"That is what assistants are for," he would joke before taking me on whatever was nearest to us: desk, couch, counter, against the wall, or window. You get my drift, I'm sure.

Securing the last black garter on my leg, I smile at the surprise I have in store for him tonight. Faking a bad headache, I'd left early from work. Worried, he didn't want me going home alone, but with a little help from his personal assistant, he'd been kept swamped in paperwork all afternoon. I think he's texted me at least every fifteen minutes since I'd left this afternoon.

Picking up his favorite pen off his desk, I smile at the memory of what he'd had me do with it. Using it to write my note to him, I carefully place it back on top of his desk. The sweet chime of the front door opening alerts me of his arrival, so I hurry back down the hall to our bedroom.

"Blaire?" His concerned voice echoes through our dark apartment.

"Blaire, Baby, where are you?" His tone instantly softens when he reaches our room.

Warm, amber candlelight dances all around us as Chris Brown's "Sweet Love" plays softly in the background. Smiling seductively, I throw back the covers, revealing my provocative outfit. I'm wearing a black lace camisole teddy with matching boy panties, garters, and hose. His favorite black, lace-up stilettos top off my sexy ensemble. These shoes hurt like hell to stand in, but something tells me that I won't be doing much standing tonight.

Continuing with my plan, I motion with my index finger for him to come to me. Even in the candlelight, I can see his eyes darken with desire and need. Frantically, he begins jerking loose his tie while charging toward me. Leaning back across our soft bed, I spread my legs, arching my back as I slide my hand between my legs.

The weight on the bed shifts and immediately his mouth is on mine, sweetly massaging our tongues in perfect sync. He breaks our kiss and leans his forehead against mine before lightly placing a kiss on my nose.

"So does this mean you are feeling better, Mrs. Ryder?"

"I am now that you're home, Mr. Ryder," I reply and he rewards me with that killer smile of his. The one I swear should be made illegal because it's just that lethal! Staring deep into his dark chocolate eyes, I can't keep from admiring how gorgeous my husband is. It is still hard for me to believe that we've been married for a little over a month now. Not wanting a big wedding,

Jaxxon and I had decided on a simple beach wedding in Fiji. After which, we'd spent three glorious weeks there on our honeymoon. Three weeks of nothing but complete and total bliss. Three weeks of making this beautiful baby inside of me.

As I pull him down to me, the candlelight dances off his dark eyes. Kissing my neck, he gently slides his right hand up my inner thigh, making my clit throb harder.

"I missed you, Baby," he whispers in my ear before placing another gentle kiss on my neck.

"Really? How much?" I tease, making him growl in response. He hates it when I tease him. It usually lands me with a deliciously sore bottom, but I love every minute of it.

"Does Mrs. Ryder want to play?" he asks while tickling me. The man has done every imaginable thing to me, but when he tickles, I surrender!

"STOP! You're going to make me pee!" I scream through my uncontrollable laughter.

"I'd rather make you come," he breathes across my mouth. My clit throbs; my pussy drenches. The power in his voice has that instant effect on me.

"Oh, yeah?" I tease him again, but this time he grabs my hands and forces them above my head.

"Don't move them! I mean it!" he orders. I keep them in place as if they have an invisible binding on them. We play this game all the time, and I never challenge his orders. Well okay, sometimes I do. But it's only because I love the punishments he gives me. Nowadays, we make love just as much as we enjoy the harder stuff. We still use Level 9 many times a week. It's a necessity just as much for me as it is for him. Only now, we know the limits of our control. We save each other; we share a connection unlike anything I could ever desire. His demon leads me into the dark; I guide him back out to the light. He is my life, my forever.

Kissing down my jaw, he works down to my chest. My body is on fire for him. Cradling my face, he lifts up and gently licks up my lip. Catching his tongue, I bite down and he laughs at my boldness.

"Does my beautiful wife need reminding of who is in charge?" he says, biting my jaw.

I smile at his words as he keeps working his way down my chest, pulling the strap of my camisole down on one arm to engulf my engorged breast in his mouth. Jaxxon relentlessly bites down hard on my nipple, sending waves of pleasure through my body as he twists my other one through the lace. The friction of the rough lace against my breast only enhances the erotic sensation. Throwing my head back, I moan, reveling in the rough movements on my chest.

He tenderly edges his fingers at the top lace of my boy shorts. When he reaches further down, he discovers how soaked I already am for him. He makes me this way. I am always ready for my demon, for my lover.

"Jesus! You are dripping, Baby!" he says against my skin.

"I want you," I whisper and he moans.

Pulling up my dark lace teddy, he leans down to place a soft kiss just above my mound, inching his way up to my navel. And then he stops. I hear his breath hitch and I smile. He has seen his surprise.

"Blaire? Oh my God," he gasps. His fingertips lightly trace over the words written on my stomach.

Hi Daddy!

"Well? What do you think, Daddy?" I ask, nervously waiting for his reply. We've discussed having kids, just not this soon.

"We're having a baby?" he asks, his face still in complete shock.

Oh, no! He's not happy!

"Yes, Sweetheart. We're having a baby. The doctor confirmed it this afternoon. That's where I went after I left the office. I wanted to make sure before I surprised you. I'm sorry. I know all of this is happening, maybe too soon," I reply, hanging my head.

Lifting my chin, he caresses my cheek with his other hand and smiles before placing both of them on my face. I reach up and set my hands on top of his, locking eyes with my beautiful husband's adoring gaze.

"I love you, Blaire Ryder." He kisses my lips tenderly and then releases my face. Moving down to my belly, his warm lips press against my skin, directly over where I had written the words.

"I love you, Baby Ryder. But you'd better cover your ears. I'm going to make your mommy scream awfully loud," he says to my stomach before lifting his dark, heated eyes back to mine. The love and desire in his stare is my undoing.

"Time to play, Mrs. Ryder," he growls, holding his hand out to take mine.

And with that my sweet demon surfaces, showing me that there is light even in the dark. Our love story is our own modern day fairytale. Jaxxon Alexander Ryder has officially become my Ultimate Climax and my Happily FOREVER After.

~The End~

A VERY SPECIAL NOTE FROM SEXXA

Hello My Loves! Thank you so very much for reading my book. Please leave me a review! Erotica has always been both captivating and beautiful to me. When I originally wrote Climax, I thought I was finished telling my story, but a funny thing happened. Honey started screaming in my ears, demanding to be heard. And so, I am thrilled to introduce her story…Dominate.

Sexxa

ABOUT SEXXA KOHL

USA TODAY BESTSELLING AUTHOR

Sexxa Kohl is a sexy sassy Southern bitch who ADORES sex. DUH! Her favorite hobbies include burning up the sheets with her delicious husband, achieving multiple screaming orgasms in new and unusual places, and flashing her tits to the world. She proudly admits to having a tiny bit of male eye candy addiction (Okay, she's a total man- candy whore).

Sexxa both embraces and expresses her natural sexuality fully in her writing. It is her dream to, one day, stage a massive intervention for the boring prudes of the world who believe the missionary position is erotic.

"SEEK HELP IMMEDIATELY" she screams!

Sexxa resides outside Nashville with her hot husband and their massive collection of sex toys. She aspires to spice up your world and dampen your panties.

Sexxa

Sexxa would LOVE to hear from you!

Email: authorsexxakohl@gmail.com
Facebook:
Personal Page: www.facebook.com/sexakohlauthor
Fan Page: www.facebook.com/sexakohl
Twitter: www.twitter.com/sexxakohl
Goodreads:
https://www.goodreads.com/author/show/7741727.Sexxa_Kohl

CLIMAX PLAYLIST

Climax- Usher
Do What You Want –Lady Gaga
Angel- Massive Attack
Trading Spaces-Usher
Peaches and Cream-112
S&M-Rihanna
Pour it Up-Rihanna
Love More-Chris Brown Featuring Nicki Minaj
Wicked Games- The Weeknd
Closer-Kings of Leon
Closer-Nine Inch Nails
Ride-Ciara Featuring Ludacris
My Chick Bad-Ludacris Featuring Nicki Minaj
Little Freak-Usher Featuring Nicki Minaj
Gorilla- Bruno Mars
Without Me- Fantasia Featuring Kelly Rowland & Missy Elliot
Ayo Technology-50 cent Featuring Justin Timberlake
Candyshop- 50 cent Featuring Olivia
Motivation- Kelly Rowland Featuring Lil' Wayne
Madness- Muse
Russian Roulette- Rhianna
Supermassive Big Hole- Muse
Wait-The Whisper Song- Ying Yang Twins
Porn Star Dancing-My Darkest Days
Sex on Fire- Kings of Leon
Personal Jesus- Marilyn Manson
Justify My Love- Madonna
Hold on, We're Going Home-Drake featuring Majid Jordan
Power is Mine-Lords of Acid
Control-Puddle of Mudd
Casual Sex-My Darkest Days
Talk Dirty- Jason Derulo featuring 2 Chainz
Demons-Imagine Dragons
Precious Part One- Vargo
Replay- Zendaya